ISLAND REVELATION

The Island Series Book 1

Dove Devereaux

ISLAND REVELATION
By Dove Devereaux

First edition published May 2021
ISBN No: 978-1-9168722-1-9

For enquiries, contact the publisher at www.dovedevereaux.com

CHAPTER 1

"Oh my goodness it's wonderful, absolutely marvellous. Your best yet!"

The woman standing beside Tara Hemsworth clapped her hands enthusiastically, before moving forward to consider the work more closely.

"Don't touch!" Tara shouted, making her older companion jump back.

"Sorry, I didn't mean to startle you, it's just that I added some finishing touches a few hours ago, so the oil's still wet."

"A few hours ago?" Annabel looked astonished.

Tara shrugged.

"I reviewed them all day yesterday and that dragged into the evening and then the early hours. What can I say? I wanted to make sure that the pieces I'd chosen were as good as they could be."

"Well, whatever you've done has paid off. It's perfect, absolutely perfect."

Tara cocked her head to one side; her long hair hanging down like a golden curtain. She wanted to take a little more time before she gave her verdict.

"You know there is no such thing as perfect," she said.

She could see a section of the sea, where the waves reached the shoreline that she'd spent long hours working on and now she was satisfied. The deadline of the exhibition had seen her reviewing each painting in turn, checking the frame worked, seeing if there were any little finishing touches that she could make. It had taken a lot of work.

'But who am I kidding, I still would've left it until the last minute,' she thought.

"Annabel's right, *Island Dawn* is your best work to date," the tall, blond man who was standing the other side of her finally spoke.

Tara lifted her head and smiled.

"I think Chris, that you two being my best friends does mean you're a little biased."

"Modest as always but even you must be able to see it, Tara."

Chris hadn't taken his eyes off the painting but he instinctively reached across and took her hand in his, giving it a squeeze. They continued to hold hands comfortably.

Tara narrowed her big brown eyes. Even if Chris and Annabel were right in their assessment, she couldn't stand big headedness.

"I suppose it's OK…" she ventured modestly.

"OK? OK? Tara, it's a masterpiece! It's stunning and everyone's going to fall in love with it…and with you," Annabel smiled up at her tall young friend.

Tara reached out and squeezed her shoulder gratefully, then withdrew her hand in shock, snatching her other hand out of Chris's at the same time.

"Oh my goodness you two, I'm so sorry, I'm still covered in paint! I hope I haven't got any on your new dress Annabel?"

"I don't think so," Annabel examined the pretty material where Tara had rested her hand.

"No, no harm done but it wouldn't have mattered if there was – I could claim to be a part of this beautiful painting. A part of the artwork from one of the rising stars in the industry."

"Well it's lovely of you to say so. I just hope it plays its part in helping the island. I owe this place so much," Tara's eyes suddenly glistened with tears.

She wasn't exaggerating, when she first came to Tresco half a decade ago, she was a shadow of her former self, afraid and lacking in confidence. Kindly Annabel, 30 years her senior, had immediately taken the young artist under her wing and since then the island had become her sanctuary, the sea acting as a wall against the outside world. Later, Chris had come into her life, giving her much needed skills as he sought to help her regain confidence. Thanks to their love and kindness she'd flourished and this was reflected in her ever-improving paintings.

Now she had friends, a beautiful home and was able to support herself doing the thing she loved the most. More than just support herself as it turned out; her work was increasingly sought after across the world and was fetching excellent prices.

"Just to check, you're happy to meet one or two key

donors this evening but still no interviews with the press?" ventured Annabel cautiously.

"You know what her answer's going to be," Chris said flatly.

He knew Annabel meant no harm but Tara could detect the slight irritation in his tone.

"I know, I know, the answer is no," Annabel sighed, tucking a stray grey hair behind her ear.

"You can't blame me for trying though, surely? I mean our very own Monet right here under our noses and such a lovely person too; we really want to brag about you to everyone we meet."

"That's very sweet of you," Tara put an affectionate arm around Annabel, careful not to touch her with painty hands this time. She squeezed her lightly.

"But you know I can't…it would unleash…too much…"

Her mind immediately flashed back to the summer five years ago, feeling the strength of his arms as he lowered her gently onto the sand, that sense of powerlessness as his kiss consumed her, the way they both had to fight their desire to take things further. That was until the betrayal, the lie that she could never recover from. She shuddered and forced herself back to the present. Her simple, uncomplicated world.

"Besides, it probably adds to their value doesn't it? That air of mystery surrounding the artist, not knowing who created it? Sort of like a second Banksy – although I'm not that big a mystery because actually you can visit me in my studio, if you can be bothered to make the trip here."

"And plenty of people are making that trip later this

evening. It really is quite the guest list."

"Hmmmnnn I'm sure." Tara didn't want to know any of the details.

Tonight's event was important for her friends on the island as they sought to create new markets for the tourism businesses that they all relied on so heavily for their income. She would do everything she could to help but the thought of an evening where she had to swap her overalls for glad rags, be on her best behaviour, talk politely to people she'd never met and would never see again, filled her with dread. Still, it was only a few hours – what difference could that make to her life?

"Are you sure you don't want me to come with you?"

Tara looked at Chris and saw his face was etched with concern. Though he needn't be – he had taught her well.

"No, really don't worry. It's just one evening, everything's going to be fine. But thank you."

"I can go you through the details with you, if you'd like?" Annabel persisted.

"Tell you what, why don't we leave it as a surprise. In the meantime, I'd better head back and see Delilah and then get dolled up. After I get the rest of this paint off my hands."

With that Tara gave each of her friends a quick kiss on the cheek and headed out of the door. As she walked along the lane towards home, her heart was as light as her steps. It was a good piece of work, Annabel and Chris were right. Not as perfect as they seemed to think it was but it was good. The more secure she felt here, the more her artistic abilities seemed to be growing. She did a little jump over the speed bump which was in the road to slow the speed of the few drivers on the island. It had become a little ritual for her to skip over it, chiefly because in her new life, this was the only bump in the road.

CHAPTER 2

"One Caffe Latte and they had your favourite cake there too...you know, the one named after me."

Sam Kerchavel placed the steaming drink and the carefully wrapped cake onto the desk in front of Mel, his PA. She looked up and gave him a huge smile.

"Wow, millionaire's shortbread, thank you. And it's so lovely to have a treat to myself for once without little pleading faces watching me!"

It was hard to believe that Mel and her husband James had welcomed their third child just a few months ago. Despite the sleepless nights and the chaos of having three children under 5 to take care of, by all accounts they were still as in love as they had been when they first met at high school. Sam was just glad to have the opportunity to treat his loyal, hard-working PA; things were so busy he didn't often get the chance.

"So remind me, did we decide in the end that I would overnight it in Manchester ready to deliver the speech at that conference tomorrow, or go early in the morning? I know you have it all organised."

"Ah…about that…" Mel spread her hands apologetically and gave him a wry smile. "There's been a bit of a change of plan. John's going to deliver the speech on your behalf and I've cleared your diary for a few days."

"Cleared my diary?" Sam raised an eyebrow.

There was only one woman in the world who could clear his diary and get away with it. Actually, in the past there were two women who he would drop all his other commitments for without a second thought and he was struck by the sudden pang of pain which still lingered. He quickly pushed the feeling away. Today, there was only one woman who had that sort of say over his arrangements.

"And do you know what my mother has planned for me?"

"Haven't got a clue," laughed Mel. "But she did ask me to get you to call her as soon as you got back."

Sam pressed the number on his phone and it was ringing by the time he reached the broad, walnut desk in his office. He sat down in the chair and waited impatiently for the call to be answered. Despite his banter with Mel, it was rare for his mother to be so demanding and he couldn't help but be concerned.

"Mum, is everything OK?"

"Of course darling, everything's fine."

"And Nick's OK?"

"Absolutely."

Sam felt his shoulders relax a little. He was just as worried about the health of his beloved stepfather as he was for his mother.

"Mel says you've cleared my diary."

"Ah yes, she's a great girl is Mel. The thing is Sam, I have to go away for a couple of days for an event. It's a charity that I've been asked to consider supporting. Nick was going to go but something urgent has come up and so I have no-one to go with."

"Well, if your husband can't make it, can't one of your lunch gang go with you? I'm pretty pushed at the moment."

"Would you believe, not one of them is available!"

'No,' thought Sam, picturing the faces of her many friends: 'I wouldn't believe that.'

His mother obviously had plans for him. Question was, what?

"Besides, I hardly ever get to spend time on my own with you anymore and will have even less opportunity to do that soon, if you ever get around to setting a date. It will be lots of fun and the weather forecast is very good, which will make it idyllic – glittering sea, beautiful islands…"

Sam looked through the smoked glass of his window, which towered above most of the other neighbouring office blocks. From where he stood he had an outstanding view, right across the city of London.

"Sea? Islands? Where on earth are we going?"

He spoke as if the trip was already a fait accompli, which it was. He and his mother had endured many trials over the years and while he would never have wished it to be so tough, it had given them an unbreakable bond. There was nothing in the world he wouldn't do for her, including accompanying her on a random trip somewhere far off shore.

"The Isles of Scilly, that's where we're heading. Just off Lands End, you know, Cornwall. Mel tells me there's a derelict hotel that you wanted to look at in Newquay and so she'll arrange for you to see that on the way back. So to all intents and purposes it's a business trip, just with a short detour beforehand. The helicopter is ready to go and I'll be with you in…"

With that the door to Sam's office opened and his mother walked in, still holding her phone to her ear and laughing.

"Mum!"

Sam cut the call and hurried forward. The pair hugged for a long time. Despite being a tall and elegant woman, the top of her head only reached to his shoulder. There was no mistaking they were mother and son; both shared the same piercing blue eyes and while Elizabeth's hair was now peppered with silver, it was otherwise raven dark like her son's.

They finally separated and he could see his mother's eyes glistening.

"Right then, shall we go?" she said matter-of-factly, though unable to disguise the emotion in her voice at seeing her son.

"OK."

Sam had built a successful business on always being ready to move quickly on a deal, to travel at short notice in order to shake hands on it if needs be. To do this he always had two bags in the office which were packed and ready to go. One contained winter gear, the other cooler clothing for warmer climes. Until now it meant he was always ahead of the opposition, although puzzlingly he had missed out on a couple of contracts recently. He shook the thought away.

"I'm guessing I won't need my ski jacket," he laughed, grabbing his holdall and picking up a suit bag on the way. He gave Mel a mock salute as he passed and followed his mother to the lift. He could already make out the whirl of his private helicopter on the roof of the building. Mel must have arranged it all. He must remember to pick up some gifts for her children while he was away; he was proud Godfather to her second son, Jacob, but he always made sure he treated them all equally. Besides, he enjoyed picking out gifts that he thought they would love.

The helicopter quickly left the dense city behind and was soon racing over the green fields of England. Sam always felt a tug whenever he travelled across the countryside. While his business was based in London he had been brought up in the country and it was in his heart, a part of his soul. Much as he loved Manchester and was looking forward to what promised to be a stimulating conference, the thought of a few days by the sea was growing on him.

Sam had never been to the Isles of Scilly and as they drew closer he straightened up in his seat. He could scarcely believe they were still in England, looking onto silken white beaches and azure waters which surrounded rocky outcrops and larger islands below. It was as if they were flying over the Caribbean. Without warning he suddenly found himself wishing he could have brought Tamara here because she would have loved it. But what a ridiculous thought! Time had washed against those sands too many times to continue to look back. Besides, he had no idea where she was, despite looking high and low for her for years. It was as if she had vanished into the white fluffy clouds above them. Finally, heartbroken, he had realised that she didn't want him to find her and with that realisation he had built a fortress around his own heart, to which only his mother had the key.

The helicopter started its descent above one of the larger islands and Sam could make out scatterings of sweet cottages tucked into coves and hillsides surrounding sweeping sands. Some sort of stately home came into view and they touched down on a large area of grass which acted as a landing pad, just to the side of it.

"Tresco," his mother declared triumphantly as the rotor blades came to a stop. "I've not been here for a long, long time."

"I didn't know you'd been here at all," Sam jumped out of the helicopter and turned to offer his hand. She didn't need it but took it anyway.

"Oh yes, my parents brought us here once when we were children. I can't remember too many details, other than a lingering sense of its beauty."

Sam was about to ask more when a tall straight-backed man, with neat grey hair and wearing a grey flannel suit, stepped towards them.

"Lady Rathers, I'm Don Symonds, one of the Chairs of the charity. We spoke on the phone. Thank you so much for coming."

"Yes of course, I'm very pleased to meet you. And please, call me Elizabeth."

They shook hands.

Not for the first time Sam was struck by how formal his mother's name was. He hardly ever heard Lady Rathers used, or even Elizabeth – Nick simply called his wife Lily.

"And this is my son, Sam Kerchavel."

Don Symonds turned to look at him and his jaw almost hit the floor as he recognised the famous tycoon.

"Of Kerchavel Holdings?"

"That's right," Sam too held out his hand. Don took it and shook it heartily.

"We're very glad that you could spare the time, given how busy you are."

Sam was tempted to say that he'd had little choice in the matter but knew that would appear ungracious. Instead, he merely smiled and followed Don as he led them away from the helipad.

"I've arranged for your bags to go straight to your accommodation but I thought you might welcome some refreshments and so I've organised afternoon tea in one of our innovative new galleries which has been set up for the fundraiser tonight. We are blessed with a wide range of talent, including work by one of our most celebrated artists," explained the older man as he walked.

Sam really felt like checking into his room, getting out of his suit and enjoying a quick burst under a refreshing shower. The September sun still packed a punch and if his mum was OK for an hour or two he wanted to make the most of it by exploring the beaches and getting a swim in before the event that evening. He also had a call to make, if only to avoid a row later on. That thought didn't fill him with much pleasure but for now duty called and he sat at the back of the golf buggy as Don drove them through the narrow lanes of the stunning island.

Sam was no horticulturalist – a lack of time meant he employed gardeners for his Windsor home, but even he could appreciate the lushness of the flora surrounding them; the swaying palm trees, the giant ferns, the unusual blooms that wouldn't have looked out of place in South America or the Mediterranean.

He was still taking everything in as they came to a gentle stop. They were near a quiet cove, which was home to half a dozen stone cottages, backing onto the gentle aqua waters.

"We've arranged for you to stay in the furthest cottage and fortunately there are two rooms," Don waved a hand in the general direction. "I'm sorry they might not be quite what you're used to – not five star but they are very comfortable and an authentic reflection of the island."

"Not at all," said Sam. "They look perfect."

Sam felt a frisson of excitement. Property had always interested him, even as a small boy. Probably because they'd had to move around so much, often bolting in the middle of the night thanks to his father's penchant for the bottle and the horses. It left Sam with a desire for the security that bricks and mortar could provide. Nowadays when he travelled he stayed in luxurious suites in the world's top hotels but they no longer held his interest. Sure, there was every luxury that money could buy, but he often longed for a simpler existence. Perhaps that explained why he was so taken with the row of stone cottages, standing solid to resist the storms which surely came to these parts in winter, yet today glowing warm in the late summer sunshine, their white-washed gateways adorned with local shells.

Don and his mother had stepped down from the cart and Sam followed them to the first cottage, up the paved path to the wide, low front door. He had to duck to avoid banging his head as he stepped inside.

"Oh this is gorgeous!" his mother exclaimed.

The whole of the downstairs had been transformed into a gallery, the entrance hall awash with glittering pots and vases, which were set back into the alcoves of the windows and placed along a long, rough wooden table running the whole length of the space. Sam had been taught by his mother to appreciate the work and skill that went into works of art and he was glad to study them closely for a few moments, despite still itching to sample the blue waters which glistened beyond the cottage's windows.

Don ushered them from one room to the next and Sam couldn't help but admire the ingenious way this small charity, designed to help promote the local arts and crafts of the islands, had transformed this cottage into a dynamic exhibition space. He felt inclined to invest in it himself at the fundraiser that evening.

Finally, they reached a thick oak door and Don turned towards them as if about to unveil a huge secret. He even put a finger to his lips briefly, even though it was just the three of them there. Sam swallowed down a smile.

"This room has been dedicated to our most talented

artist; certainly our most popular. Her work is starting to attract international interest and she has been generous enough to donate some of it to supporting our cause. I'm sure you'll agree that it is truly wonderful."

Although the door remained closed, Sam had already made up his mind. There was only one artist who he would ever describe as 'truly wonderful' and she was long gone from his life. No one would ever be able to match her. Even so, he was intrigued to see the work that Don was so enthusiastic about.

Don opened the door with his arm, as if pulling back a wooden curtain to provide mother and son with a grand reveal.

Sam stepped through the entrance and his breath caught in his throat.

Don was right, the paintings which adorned all three walls were truly wonderful. Wonderful, unique, exquisite, the most astonishing work Sam had ever seen. He was immediately transported back to the time they had shared together. He had loved to watch her at her easel, especially on the occasions when she was suddenly struck by an idea and a need to paint. Her blonde eyebrows would be knitted together in concentration, those liquid brown eyes all seeing. Her brush would at one time be drawing across the canvas in large swathes, next dabbing to create the tiniest detail. Sam would sit a few feet behind her and watch in awe as the seemingly random strokes of thick glutinous oils suddenly transformed into a vision of coastal life, so real that he felt if he stepped forward into the painting he would feel the sand beneath his toes, or the coolness of waves breaking against his skin.

His reverie was broken by Don's loud cough and he turned to see himself being watched closely.

"It is divine, isn't it," Don said.

Sam nodded but found his words were stuck in his throat.

He knew her work anywhere, it was unmistakable, like a fingerprint or DNA. True, he had not seen any of her paintings for many years and he could see how her talent had grown since then but they still haunted his dreams. Sam stood and stared at the works surrounding him on each of the four walls of the room. He felt blindsided, winded. All those years searching and now he had found her quite by chance.

"Will the artist be here tonight?" he finally managed to croak, his voice in danger of giving his feelings away.

Thankfully Don didn't seem to notice.

"Oh yes," he said. "She'll be here. Would you like to meet her?"

"Oh most definitely."

That was an understatement. After she left, his search had turned from days to weeks, weeks to months and finally, months to years. At first he wanted her back so badly it was like a fire which raged through him, filling his waking hours and many of his fitful sleeping ones. Eventually he had to accept that she didn't want to be found, but for a time he still continued to search because by then it wasn't about what she wanted anymore. It was about him. He had a burning desire to get something from her; answers. Answers as to why she'd pretended she loved him. Answers as to why she'd walked out of their future together without so much as a backward glance.

And tonight he was damned well going to get them.

CHAPTER 3

Tara stepped out of the steaming shower and wrapped a large Egyptian cotton towel around herself, the cream fabric accentuating her healthy tan. She was very careful not to catch the sun and always put on cream even when it was cloudy; the glow of her skin was from years of healthy living and the positive outlook on life she'd developed over the past few years.

She tied her hair up in another towel and went across to the bay window which looked out over the little cove. The benefit of being the last in a row of cottages which were all largely holiday homes, was a private view of the sea beyond.

She could see Delilah still out in the garden, chasing a butterfly around the lawn, with no hope of catching the colourful creature. She would have to call her pet in before too long.

The small stretch of sand had emptied of visitors an hour or so before but now in the gentle glow of the summer evening, a figure was entering the water. He strode forth with strength and determination as if he was angry with the very waves which were gently lapping at the shore. As Tara watched in astonishment they seemed to yield to his will, parting so that he could dive beneath the surface.

A shiver ran through Tara; of what? Fear? Desire? Worse, recognition?

She shook herself free of the thought, pulled the towel more snugly around her body but stayed watching, mesmerised.

There was no sign of him. Would he ever surface? Her heart was in her mouth and instinctively she felt around her for her phone. Swimmers rarely got into difficulties here but it wasn't unheard of and getting help quickly by calling the Coastguard made the difference between life and death. But then…there…further out than she had imagined, the man's head and shoulders suddenly broke the surface. Even at this distance she could see his dark hair slick black, the water pouring off the contours of his muscular shoulders. It jolted her back to another memory, feeling the hardness of muscle beneath taught skin, her own strength heightened, meeting his, daring him…

Tara tore her gaze from the window. She had managed to push thoughts of Sam away for so long, locked them deep into her soul, so she was shocked at the impact this complete stranger had. As well as the physical stirrings which she had long thought hidden, there was that slow burning rage, the spark caused by the betrayal that had never quite been quenched. It did not do to dwell on these things, especially now.

"Focus, Tara focus. Tonight is an important night for the islanders. You can't let them down."

She pulled the curtains so that she would no longer be

tempted to watch the mysterious swimmer, who had encouraged thoughts of Sam to rise within her like a tidal wave. Instead, she headed back to the bathroom to start on her make-up and hair. Her face was flushed, her eyes bright.

"This is going to take a bit of work," she said to her reflection with a faint smile.

In reality she knew she never needed much make-up. Some mascara, a dab of lipstick and a little powder always made her look as if she spent six hours with a make-up artist to the Hollywood stars. Suddenly on a whim, she slid open the drawer beneath her mirror and took out the small velvet box. Hands shaking, Tara opened it for the first time in five years, ever since the day she had dropped it into her bag which she had then slung over her shoulder, before closing the flat door behind her for the last time.

The stone immediately caught what light there was in the room. It was beautiful, exquisite, perfect and once again, took her breath away. She quickly snapped the box shut and slammed the drawer closed. It really did no good to dwell on the past. No good at all. With a heavy sigh she reached across and picked up her mascara.

*****

Sam surfaced from beneath the waters and shook the droplets from his face. He was struggling with his emotions, maybe this wasn't such a good idea. He was a powerful swimmer but also had total respect for the sea and he didn't know these waters. He knew that being distracted could prove fatal no matter how good you were.

But he was finding it hard to concentrate through the whirlwind of thoughts. He was still reeling from the shock of seeing her work. He had dreamt of this moment for years. When Tamara first disappeared, he had searched high and low across the world until exhausted and demoralised he had to face defeat. It was the only thing that had ever beaten him.

It was as if she had vanished, a beautiful ghost who had touched his heart and forever left her mark on him. On the third anniversary of her leaving he decided to end his search and close his heart forever; he could not afford to let anyone get that close again. He had known the height of ecstasy, physically and emotionally and while he sometimes missed those feelings, he had barely survived the rawness of the grief that followed. He would not go through that again.

So then to stumble across her by chance like this…

"As if it was fate," he murmured, as his face broke the waves again. He thought of his mother. As far as he knew, she and Tamara had never met but he wouldn't put it past her to have some involvement in this.

He had recovered himself quite quickly when he first came across her work that afternoon in the gallery. It was like a double punch to the guts, to have found her but also to have been faced with the stunning art that she had created. They were literally breath-taking – her scenes as real as the water he was now tearing through.

"Is the artist local then?" he had asked Don, hoping his voice didn't betray him.

"She is indeed. A very popular member of our community."

So she lived here too.

Satisfied, Sam made an excuse about a business call and headed to his apartment, changing quickly and heading off in search of the nearest beach.

Despite his strength in the water he found his arms felt shaky and his body cold, even though the sea was at its warmest at this time of year.

He wanted answers from Tamara as to why she had left him so suddenly and without a trace, when he had given her everything - it was the least he deserved. And finally, within the next few hours he would have them.

CHAPTER 4

"So this is where you've been hiding."

Tara spun round and found herself staring into the handsome face of her former fiancé, Sam Kerchavel.

He stood a whole head height above her, his dark hair cropped short and accentuating the exquisite navy suit he was wearing; a suit which seemed to be wrestling with the muscled body beneath. His blue eyes were as cold as ice and when they met hers, she shuddered.

She was so astonished that the elegant glass of champagne she was holding slid from her grasp and hit the slate floor with a loud crash, splintering into a million tiny pieces.

The room went quiet and thirty pairs of eyes turned to look at the handsome pair.

"Sorry, sorry, not sure what happened there," Tara said apologetically and she dropped to her haunches to start to clear up the mess, taking care not to let the deep red silk of her dress get soaked with the spilt champagne.

At least people would think that her blushes were caused by the accident with the glass and not the fact that Sam Kerchavel had just walked back into her life, like some sort of unwanted phantom. What was he doing here!?

"Here, let me help."

Sam dropped down next to her and also began gathering shards. The conversation around the room started to pick up again and was soon back to normal levels, giving Tara a chance to speak, without being overheard.

"What are you doing here Sam?" she hissed.

"I could ask you the same thing."

"I…I…live here."

"So I gather. Good place to hide."

"Hide? I'm not hiding."

Tara tilted her chin defiantly. How dare he come in and accuse her like this! He was the one who had lied, ripped the trust out of their relationship, giving her no option but to flee.

Furious, she scraped at some of the glass that was lying in a pool of the champagne just in front of her.

"Ouch!"

A shard of glass caught her hand and almost immediately the blood came.

"Be careful! Here, let me look."

Quick as a flash, Sam took her hand in his, the warmth of his skin causing a jolt to pass through her body. She swallowed hard and focussed instead on the wound.

"It's quite deep," he told her.

Was it her imagination or was his voice full of concern? A bit different from how he was a few moments ago.

"I don't think it needs stitches but we do need to wash it and make sure all the glass is out and get a dressing on it. Come on, up you get."

He placed his arm gently around her slender waist, causing ripples of fire to pulse right through her. Why did he not seem to notice, was he not affected in the same way? Instead, he eased her back up to a standing position as if nothing had happened. Slightly overcome by his sudden presence and the cut on her hand she swayed against him and could smell the dizzying mix of his aftershave and the rawness of his own scent. It was far more intoxicating than any champagne.

"Steady now, easy."

Don, the exhibition organiser rushed over to them.

"Oh my goodness, Tara are you alright?"

"Tara?" Sam raised an eyebrow.

"Yes, Tara, Tara Hemsworth. She's the artist behind all of these magnificent works; the person you were so keen to meet."

"Keen to meet, eh?" Tara couldn't help but question Sam. He had the good grace to look away awkwardly.

'So exactly how long has Sam known I was here?' Tara thought to herself grimly. She knew that her work was a giveaway, he would have recognised it immediately. Her style had changed a little and her technique had been transformed but the essence of it was still there. And why after all this time was he able to set her heart racing in precisely three seconds flat?

'Don't forget what he did to you,' a voice in her head reminded her firmly.

"The kitchen area is just through here," Don bustled ahead of them and Sam, still gently supporting her and cupping her injured hand, started to guide her through the crowd of people.

"It's fine, I can manage on my own," Tara tried to sound independent but in fact she was quite shaken.

"Not a problem."

She thought 'not a problem' might mean he was going to let her go but there was no sign of his loosening his arm around her waist and he continued to guide her towards Don.

They reached the kitchen, which was bustling with islanders who had been drafted in to help out with the evening and were busy pouring more champagne into glasses and stocking silver platters with delicious homemade canapes. Many of them greeted Tara like an old friend as she arrived.

"Through here," said Don and led them to a far corner of the room which had a table and a couple of chairs, with jackets and coats covering them. He pulled some off and placed them carefully on another part of the table. Behind them was a low sink and Sam took her straight to it, setting the water going with his elbow. Tentatively, Tara put her bloodied hand beneath the flow. It stung and she gasped with pain.

"Here, let me see, you might have some glass in it still."

Sam took her hand once again and lowered his head towards it to examine it more closely. Tara stared at the nape of his neck, with its dark short hair and a memory flashed back into her mind. It was the summer, just the two of them in a battered retro campervan…hitting the coast. He was behind the wheel, frowning in concentration as he took the van down increasingly narrow lanes, while she stroked the back of his neck thoughtfully, then playfully, thinking of the time when his concentration would be fully on her instead, his tongue seeking and finding hers, the closeness of his embrace.....

"Ouch!"

She was grateful for the pain which brought her back to reality.

"There. Got it."

"Er...thanks."

The pain was swiftly gone. Sam was starting to stand up straight again, peering at a sharp shard of glass that he held between his thumb and forefinger.

"Sorry if that hurt, but it was important to remove it and it should start to feel better now. One more rinse and then we can dress it," he turned to look at her and their eyes locked. Dark brown pools met blue ice and passion raged through her veins, like a re-awakened volcano. There was no mistaking it, the unquenchable heat between them was still there, even after all these years. Even after all the betrayal and heartache.

'But that's all it is, desire,' she told herself firmly and tore her gaze away from his.

"Oh my dear, you're shaking, do you want to sit down?" Don was bustling back with the first aid kit, his face etched with concern.

"No, no I'm fine it's just the water...it's cold and my hand is sore."

Tara was glad that she could cover up her true feelings with her injury. What was Sam doing here? Why had he suddenly walked back into her well-ordered life? She had spent the last five years doing all she could to forget this man who had stolen her heart before breaking it into a million pieces. She had felt that her love and passion was matched only by his, until the day he had lied to her face. It had swept away her very foundations, as she had realised she couldn't trust him. Did it mean his love for her had been a lie too?

Don passed her a clean towel and she immediately snatched her hand away from Sam's grasp and used her other hand to wrap the cloth around the cut.

Sam looked at her with surprise but said nothing. Instead, he started to rummage in the first aid kit that Don had laid on the counter beside them. He was looking for an antiseptic wipe and a dressing but while the items were right in front of him, he couldn't immediately see them because his mind was in tatters. For the remainder of his swim and the time it had taken to shower the salt from his body and get dressed for the evening he had rehearsed what he was going to say. He had tried to imagine what it would be like to see her for the first time in half a decade.

He had been jittery all the way to the exhibition.

"Are you alright?"

His mother had scanned his face quizzically as they'd headed towards the gallery earlier that evening.

"Of course. Why wouldn't I be?"

"No reason, no reason at all," she shot him a sideways look. "And that's why it's odd."

"Oh well you know, just a couple of work things on my mind."

"What sort of things?"

Sam had regretted saying it as soon as the words were out of his mouth. He had tried to protect his mother ever since he was old enough to; first physically and then financially until she met the kind and dynamic Nick Rathers. She had done the same for Sam and even though he had despised the hardships they had faced before his career blossomed and his beloved stepfather arrived on the scene, it had created an incredible closeness between mother and son. So to have hinted at something troubling him would not have gone unnoticed. But to his astonishment and relief she'd made no further comment, though he'd been extra cautious when they'd arrived at the gallery. He had greeted Don and the other exhibition organisers as politely as he could, whilst trying to subtly scan the room for Tamara.

'Where is she, damn it?' he had said to himself, refusing another glass of champagne from the overzealous waitress.

'Maybe she knows I'm here?'

It was possible. His mother was the main guest but her entrepreneurial son was bound to have set some tongues wagging and he couldn't help but notice how some of the women in the room gave him lingering smiles as he went past. Perhaps news had reached Tamara and she'd decided not to attend after all. It didn't seem like her to let her local community down though, she was always so generous, so caring.

'But then again, for some reason she got up and left me

one day without so much as a goodbye. Then went to great lengths to make sure she wasn't found,' he thought grimly. 'So maybe I didn't really know her at all.'

And then suddenly, like dawn lifting after a stormy night, he caught a fleeting glimpse of a sheen of golden hair, which dazzled in the light of the room. Without the need for her to turn around, he knew it was Tamara. Clutching his glass more tightly, he had made his way quickly through the crowded room, as if nothing else in the world mattered, oblivious to everyone else he passed. It was as if the gallery had been cleared of everybody but her.

It hadn't occurred to him that his heart would skip a beat as he stared into her lovely face, or how anguished he would feel when she cut her hand. But the injury she had caused his heart had been far more painful, a cut so deep that he'd never totally healed. He realised that now.

Now she was nursing her hand and glaring at him defiantly.

"Are you planning on telling me what you're doing here?" she hissed into his ear as he wiped the cut with the antiseptic wipe.

"I could ask you the same thing, Tamara," he spat back, his voice as quiet as hers so as not to attract attention.

"Or should I say Tara? By the way, which is your name? In fact, what about you is actually real?"

He heard her suck in her breath with shock at his words and turned his face towards her.

Her huge brown eyes had widened for a moment before narrowing. A memory flashed into his mind, that night camping near the moors, the light of their bonfire dancing in her eyes. If he'd had to he would have dashed through those very flames to reach her, the heat of the fire nothing in comparison with his burning love for her and the need to have her by his side.

Sam shut the memory out. That was a very different time, maybe one that had never really existed except in his own mind….and heart. A sudden burst of anger, borne of heartache washed over him.

"You owe me an explanation."

"I owe *you*!"

"Yes, you owe me. You were my *fiancée*," Sam ground out the word through gritted teeth.

"We were happy together, were going to get married and spend the rest of our lives together – at least that was the impression you gave. Maybe you were just a very good actress, luring me in until a better offer came along…."

He heard her sharp intake of breath again but he had five years of pent up hurt and rage spilling out and he wasn't about to concern himself with her feelings.

"….was that it Tara? Another man? A better offer? Or maybe just a rare fit of conscience – realising that this game of yours was a bit serious after all and that you might actually hurt someone. Which was it? Come on, do tell – you owe me that at least."

"Is everything alright Tara?"

Sam spun around to come face to face with a blond, stocky man. He was only a couple of inches shorter and stood eyeball to eyeball with him. Sam stiffened and faced the stranger head on, only flinching a little as he saw Tara reach across and touch the man gently on the arm.

"It's fine Chris, just fine. Sam and I are….are…well we're old friends. That's all."

Old friends? Is that what he had been relegated to? Sam's jaw tightened as he held the other man's gaze.

"Old friends? Didn't look that way to me."

"That? Oh, we were just messing around. You know, for old times' sake."

Sam could detect the tension in Tara's voice and suspected the other man could too, though he softened his stance a little at her words.

Who was he? Her lover? Husband? Sam didn't really know what women went for but he supposed this man was handsome, even with his crooked nose that looked like the result of a rugby accident. Plus his blue eyes seemed a little too close together for Sam's liking. The question was, what did Tara see in him - what was this man to her? A lump formed in Sam's throat and he turned to Tara expectantly.

"Chris this is Sam. Sam, Chris."

That was it? Just names? No further explanation?

"I dropped my glass like an idiot, then cut my hand as I tried to clear up the mess. Sam was just helping me to clean up the blood. But I'm fine now and should really be getting back to the other guests. Chris, will you come with me?"

"Of course."

The blond man stared at Sam defiantly for just a moment longer, as if daring him to do something about it, before turning to Tara and offering her his arm. She tucked hers into his and headed back towards the party without glancing back, but feeling Sam's eyes following her as she went.

For the rest of the evening and on the journey home she stuck to Chris like glue. She saw Sam across the room now and then but he didn't seem to look at her again and as the guests thinned out towards the end of the event, she could no longer see him. Despite the nature of their meeting, she couldn't help but feel a little disappointed. As she and Chris walked back across the island to her cottage, she glanced across the moonlit sea and remembered the swimmer she had seen earlier when she had stepped out of the shower. No wonder his taught body and strength through the waves had reminded her so much of her former fiancé; she was now convinced it had been Sam she had seen. As she drew the other curtains after Chris had left to go home, Tara couldn't help but feel glad that Sam was on the same island – despite all that had happened between them. He had always had that effect on her, as if all was well with the world when he was nearby. It was good to know that he was OK, doing well by all accounts.

Though there was no way she owed him an explanation. If he hadn't twigged that she had uncovered his lies, well tough. Now that the fundraising event was over, there was no need for them to meet again and hopefully he would be getting back on a helicopter or boat in the morning and heading home, out of her life forever.

Then she remembered the look of determination on his face as he demanded answers from her. If there was one thing Tara knew about Sam Kerchavel, it was that he never gave up.

“Some chance that he’s going home anytime soon then,” she said to herself as she switched off her bedside light, ahead of a sleepless night.

CHAPTER 5

"You're never going to believe this," Annabel scuttled from behind the counter as Tara entered the gallery the next morning, rubbing what little sleep she'd had from her eyes. Delilah trotted behind her.

"Believe what?"

"Believe what happened last night."

An image of Sam, handsome in his tailored navy suit, gently washing the blood from her hand flashed into Tara's mind. Right on cue her hand throbbed a little. She put her bag down on the chair near the counter and turned towards her friend.

"They're all sold."

"What're all sold?"

"The paintings," spluttered Annabel. "Your paintings. They're all sold."

This got Tara's attention.

"What *all* of them?"

There had been ten of her works on show last night, including the large centrepiece *Island Dawn*, which had hung above the fireplace in the gallery. The price tag had not been cheap.

"Yes all of them. Over two hundred thousand pounds. Can you believe it! Two hundred thousand!"

"Wow," Tara was seriously impressed. "And do you know who bought them?"

"Ah," Annabel fiddled with a piece of her hair. "I'm afraid they were almost all bought by donors who wished to remain anonymous. Except for *Island Dawn*. I know who bought that."

"Go on." Tara had a creeping sense she knew what the answer would be.

"Well," said Annabel, clutching her friend's arm and whispering conspiratorially, even though the only other people there were at the far side of gallery.

"It was that man you know, the one who helped you when you cut your hand. The famous businessman."

"Sam Kerchavel."

Just speaking his name sent a shiver through Tara and she wondered if her friend noticed. Seemingly not.

"Yes, that's him, Sam Kerchavel. Very taken with it, Don said. He said that when he showed it to him earlier in the afternoon he looked stunned. Almost like he'd seen a ghost. He then asked lots of questions about it and you as well. As soon as the bidding opened last night he put in an enormous bid which outstripped everyone else. What do you say to that?"

Tara didn't know quite what to say. She was puzzled that Sam had bought the work because he had seemed angry with her last night – though why he should be, she didn't know. Perhaps it was because he couldn't bear the thought of someone leaving him, even if he hadn't been invested in the relationship.

'Damaged his ego, that's why he's so furious,' she thought.

The question was, should she tell Annabel that she and Sam already knew each other? When she had fled all those years ago it was Annabel she contacted and who had offered her sanctuary with no questions asked. Over the years she had opened up a little and her friend had been nothing but kind and generous. She owed her a full explanation.

"Annabel, I really should tell you…"

"Oh look here's Chris," Annabel's attention was diverted to the tall blond man entering the gallery. He was carrying a cardboard tray with three steaming drinks.

"I got us all coffee. Thought we could do with it after an unusually late night."

It was indeed rare for them to stay up so late. That was one of the things Tara loved about living on the islands, the wholesome lifestyle. Sure, occasionally one of the islanders would throw a big party for a birthday or anniversary and the local inns were great places to huddle on a dark winter's evening, or to sit outside to soak up some late summer sun. The New Year's Eve celebrations were something else but that was about all. She had imagined last night would be a rare treat but it had given her one sleepless night already and she suspected there would be a few more over the next few days.

The buzz of a helicopter soaring overhead made her look up. Was that Sam leaving the island already? The pang of disappointment surprised her but when she looked out of the doorway at the aircraft's livery, she saw it was one of the regular flights which brought the many tourists to and from the mainland.

Tara took the steaming cup gratefully and nursed it between her hands.

"I was just telling Tara how all of her works sold last night, including *Island Dawn*," Annabel turned her attention to Chris.

"Oh really and who bought that?"

"That businessman who was there. You know, the famous one, Sam Kerchavel."

"Oh right," Chris caught Tara's eye and raised an eyebrow. To her horror she felt the heat creep into her cheeks – what would Chris make of that? She dropped her gaze to the floor.

"I thought he was rather dishy," Annabel added, oblivious to the others. "Very handsome. And rather taken with our Tara."

Tara continued to study the dark slate floor of the gallery. If only her friends knew the history between the two of them. Had she not discovered what he was really like, she could be Mrs Kerchavel now!

"I think I might just go for a quick walk on the beach as you two are here," she said suddenly. "I'm still quite tired after last night, my sore hand kept me awake. A good blast of sea air will do me good."

"Of course," said Chris, heading towards the gallery's counter. "I can put in an hour and then Annabel, can you?"

"Oh yes. Take your time, Tara, I'm in no rush today.

And Delilah can stay here with us."

Tara rubbed her dog's ears and then looked up at her friends.

"Thank you."

"Not a problem."

Sipping her coffee as she went, Tara headed out of the gallery and took the narrow pathway which led straight onto the small cove. It was such a glorious place to have an art gallery and she was thankful for it every day. No two days were ever the same by the sea, with the colours and textures changing all the time, perfect for any artist.

It was still early, most holidaymakers would be having their breakfast and so she shared the beach with just a couple of gulls, who were picking their way through the seaweed which had washed up on the high tide.

Tara crouched down and rested her coffee in the sand, before picking up a white stone with her uninjured hand. She turned it over slowly. Usually, she would be entranced by the colour, its smoothness, or the faint grey veins which ran through it. Today her mind was elsewhere.

"Was it just chance that you came here, Sam?" she said. "Or did you know I was here? And if you did know, why bother to go to all of the hassle of coming over? You could find the number for the gallery and call me if you had questions. You surely know me well enough to know that I would at least answer you."

At least she thought she would. For anyone else she'd play it straight but could she with Sam? When just the sound of that deep, gravelly voice sent her mind into a whirl of emotions, leaving her confused and unsure? And what about the deceit? She had loved him so much, deeper than she could ever have imagined possible. His betrayal had almost destroyed her; had it not been her determination to survive, it might have done. She was stronger now but hadn't banked on ever seeing Sam again. Now that she had, she knew that she had to build up her best defences to protect herself from his charms.

"But I'll be damned if I'll let him get close to me again," she stood up and kicked at some seaweed furiously.

"Wherever you are Sam, hurry up and ask me your questions. Let's get this over with, once and for all and then we can go our separate ways and get on with our lives."

*****

"I thought I might take a couple of days off, as this is such a beautiful place. It might do me good to explore the island, relax a little. What are your plans?"

Sam's mother lowered the breakfast menu and eyed her son suspiciously.

"Really? You're staying for a few days? That's not like you; I thought you'd be calling the helicopter back as soon as possible. What's changed your mind?"

"Nothing really. I've been working very hard lately and could do with a few days' break. Where better than here?"

Sam splayed his hands out, as if to emphasise his innocence.

"And it's got nothing to do with that artist Tara Hemsworth I suppose? You seemed to be deep in conversation last night."

"Don't be ridiculous, or course it's got nothing to do with her!" Sam declared, a little too defensively, before conceding:

"Though I might look her up if I'm passing that way."

His mother snorted.

"It's not a very big place so I'm sure you'll *stumble* across her gallery eventually. And given you've just bought her most expensive work, I imagine she'll be very pleased to see you. But be careful, Sam."

"What do you mean?"

"You know what I mean. Miss Hemsworth is very beautiful and obviously incredibly talented but you're already in a boat and you don't want to rock it."

Sam made a face. If his mother knew the exact reason for him going to see Tara she might view the whole thing differently. She had no idea that the two of them had history. But there was no point in telling her because he had no feelings for Tara anymore – just a wish to find out why she had treated him so badly. That would allow him to put his past firmly where it belonged and get on with his life. Yes, that was the only reason he was going to seek her out, so there was absolutely no reason to tell his mother about it; it would only worry her.

All the same, he was impatient to get moving and it was all he could do to not urge his breakfast companion to hurry up. Usually, he'd be delighted to spend some time with his mother without having to dash off to a meeting, or see a developer. And much as he loved his stepfather, it was also very rare for it to just be the two of them together again, so a welcome change. Yet Sam was itching to be free to roam the island and find Tara.

"This is lovely, spending time together, we don't often get the chance," his mother said as if reading his thoughts.

"I might stay on the island for a few more days too. Then we can spend lots of time together and I can keep an eye on you."

Sam looked up at her sharply and could see a faint trace of amusement on his mother's face. She was in her late 50s now but still a stunner, the only real sign of ageing the faint laughter lines around her eyes and the corners of her mouth. No wonder Nick had fallen for her – she was beautiful inside as well as out.

Sam settled back into his seat. He needed to relish the time spent with her and not be so keen to dash off. Tara wasn't going anywhere and he was going to be here for a couple of days, plenty of time to find her, get the answers he needed and explore the island too. He'd already called Mel and left her a message to ask her to put the Newquay appointment back a day or two.

"Shall we order more coffee?" he suggested. "It's a real treat to have a leisurely breakfast."

His mother smiled warmly and reached her hand across the table to pat his.

"Of course, that would be lovely," she said. "Although Sam."

"Yes?"

"You don't fool me. Not for one minute."

CHAPTER 6

Sam was striding back to his room when his phone rang. He glanced at it irritably, he was keen to get on, now that his mother was occupied with Don, who was delighted to have arranged a tour of the botanical gardens for her.

"Mel, I'm in a bit of a rush, can it wait?"

"Just the darndest thing Sam."

"Go on," he stopped short, ears pricked up. Mel was unflappable and so if she was flagging something to him, it was a cause for concern.

"I called Mr Clinton in Newquay, the man with the derelict hotel that you wanted to look at. I said that you might need to delay your appointment by a day or two, but he said a competitor is on his way to see it today but has already made a provisional offer."

"Really!?"

Sam was astonished. The reason he'd been so successful in business was by being quick with his deals and ensuring absolute secrecy around the properties he was looking to develop. They were chiefly old buildings which had fallen into disrepair, often stunning in their previous life but neglect had led to them being overlooked when they'd gone up for sale. His investments had to be profitable but he was also driven by a desire to restore these beautiful masterpieces to their former glories. So, when he approached the owners and shared his vision with them, they were only too pleased to keep the details under wraps in exchange for a generous deal.

"I don't understand Sam," Mel's voice suddenly seemed very far away. "This is the fourth time this has happened. I'm beginning to think we've got a leak, but who?"

Who indeed?

Mentally, Sam ran through the small group of people in his inner circle but all had been with the company for years. He trusted each of them implicitly.

"Maybe it's just a coincidence," he said but he knew in his heart of hearts that it wasn't.

It wasn't that he needed the money but it was the principle. He had always treated his team fairly and they in turn worked hard for him and for the business. Many of them were as close as family, so the thought that someone was betraying him was more than disconcerting. It was devastating.

"Let's discuss this again later," he said to Mel. "In the meantime, tell him I'd still like to come and see it with a view to making a counter offer."

He ended the call and threw on a navy t-shirt and black board shorts.

He'd noticed a bike hire place just along from his cottage and he headed straight there. It was years since he'd been on a bike and he had a wry smile on his face as he wondered what Harold, his chauffeur would make of it. A bit different from the Bentley which Harold polished until you could see your face in it and which transported Sam to the office during the week, or the Aston Martin that he used himself at the weekends.

Luckily no-one was around to see him wobble a little as he first set off on the bike. The last time he'd been on one had been with her, on that idyllic week away as they toured in the camper van, with bikes slung on the back. They had explored the lanes and woodland tracks together, sometimes side by side, other times racing each other, their laughter echoing around the remote wilderness. Then they had lain in the grass, enjoying a lavish picnic and he watched her while she did quick sketches or took photos of the beautiful scenery surrounding them, in order to work them into paintings later. He wondered if she used a bike now to get around.

'She'd probably beat me hands down in any race now,' he thought, as he followed the route around the island that the man at the bike hire place had recommended.

The old saying 'just like riding a bike' was very true and Sam was soon as sure in the saddle as he'd ever been. He made a mental note to himself to buy a new bike when he got home. It would be a great way to explore his own grounds and garden. He'd forgotten how joyous it was to travel under your own power and to feel the breeze on your face as you went.

'Not much point in being a multi-millionaire if you don't

enjoy yourself,' he thought as he sped along.

Tresco was stunning and he took his time to admire its scenery as he ploughed along. It was rich and lush, the foliage as if from another part of the planet; it certainly didn't feel as if he was still in the UK. Palm trees and large agave plants, normally native to the Americas, towered above the gentle, sand-dusted lanes which branched off here and there, heading down to little coves, or weaving into banks of sand dunes. He had asked at the bike hire place where Tara's gallery was and he was heading across the island towards it; a place called Old Grimsby.

He carried on past a farm, with its herd of rich-red coloured cattle chewing contentedly on the lush island grass. Then he rose up over a hill strewn with russet bracken and stopped for a few minutes at a place called the Old Blockhouse which was perched at the top. Sam tried to imagine the workers from the 16th century who had built this fortification using thick blocks of stone. Although the Old Blockhouse was in ruins, it had stood for hundreds of years, standing guard on the headland overlooking a small group of houses, which he guessed was his final destination.

"The construction workers of today don't know they're born," he said, mentally picturing his own hard-working team of contractors.

Sam had also stopped there for a quick breather. He spent a lot of time in the state-of-the-art gym that he had designed at his home and always finished his brutal regime with a refreshing but testing swim in his luxurious indoor pool. But the bike ride and his desire to reach Tara as soon as possible meant he needed a quick break. He gazed at the little community of homes in the distance, curving around a small beach. He could see why she would pick somewhere like this to host her art and live her life; it was absolutely perfect.

Without further ado, he kicked off again and sped down the hill towards the village and the answers that he felt sure would finally give him some peace. After today he could forget all about Tara Hemsworth forever.

'Who are you trying to kid?' said a small voice in his head.

*****

The loud, incessant barking sent Tara running from the cove towards the gallery. She'd heard parents say that they could recognise their own child's cry a mile off and she could certainly recognise Delilah's distress.

As she neared the gallery the noise died down but she didn't slow up until she burst in through the doorway.

Sam was crouching down by the counter, rubbing Delilah's ears.

"There, there girl, no need to get so upset," he was saying gently to Tara's German Shepherd dog, as he stroked her head.

"I'm not here to hurt you, or rob the place either."

Tara glanced around her. There was no-one in the gallery but no sign of Chris or Annabel either.

Sam looked up.

"I was just getting acquainted with your guard dog," he explained. "She didn't seem too happy when I tried to look out the back to see if you were here."

"So I see," Tara said evenly. "But the question that's worrying me more is where are Chris or Annabel?"

She ignored what seemed like a look of disappointment on Sam's face at the mention of Chris' name and pushed her way past the counter and into the back of the shop. Sam stood up and followed her.

"Here, let me go first – you know, just in case," he said and stepped in front of her.

She couldn't help but feel a warm glow at his protectiveness, even though it was probably just inbuilt chivalry. But there wouldn't really be something sinister going on, would there?

"Through here?" Sam asked and Tara nodded.

She found herself admiring his broad back and strong shoulders beneath the soft fabric of his t-shirt. It was intoxicating and instead Tara made herself concentrate on the matter in hand.

"Chris? Annabel? Hello?" she called.

She could make out a muffled shout as they headed towards the stock room, followed by the dog. The door was heavy because it was a climate controlled room in order to protect all of her original works. And it was currently firmly closed.

Sam moved aside so that Tara could slide back the catch and she then pushed heavily at the door. Sam couldn't help but notice her muscles beneath her cropped t-shirt. She was as slender as ever but her body was more toned, as if she'd been working out in the intervening years. Attractive. He dragged his attention away from admiring her figure to.....Annabel, who was sitting on an old oak barrel looking flustered and flushed. She jumped up when the door opened.

"Goodness, Tara I'm so sorry. I just popped in and forgot to take my key with me. I've never done that before. I remembered but as I turned around a gust of wind caught the door and that was that." She looked very apologetic.

"And I've got no mobile phone signal in here. I could hear Delilah barking and I felt terrible, I hope there wasn't a thief."

"Not really a thief, more a…a…" Tara turned towards Sam and wondered how she would describe him. Annoying ex-fiancé seemed a little harsh given he'd just forked out a lot of money for her main painting which would benefit the whole island. Though he could afford it very easily, she knew that much. She may have been living on an island for five years but she hadn't been under a rock and so was well aware of how Sam Kerchavel's fortunes had risen.

"Less thief, more interested investor," Sam picked up smoothly.

He moved across the storeroom and helped Annabel up from the barrel. Tara studied him for a moment, while his attention was taken with reassuring her anxious friend who was talking nineteen to the dozen.

Why on earth would he be interested in her career now, other than perhaps to wreak more havoc in her life than he had the first time around? Well she damn well wasn't going to allow that.

She led the way back to the main gallery, with Sam, Annabel and the dog trailing in her wake. Tara fished out a dog biscuit from a jar and called out:

"Del, Delly, come here."

The dog seemed puzzled for a moment but soon sniffed out the biscuit and came to take it gently from her hand. Tara bent down and kissed her head fondly and Sam felt a pang of envy.

'That's a first,' he thought wryly. 'I've never been jealous of a dog before.'

An apologetic Annabel busied herself making tea, giving Sam a chance to look around. It was truly stunning. Timber framed and slate floored, it had been designed with long thin floor to ceiling windows at regular intervals along two of the walls. These windows were not much bigger than the arrow slits found in old castles, affording just a slither of view of the pretty cove at the front, and bracken-laden countryside to the left. They gave the right amount of light to enhance the magnificent works along the other sections of wall and to ensure that the visitors focussed on the art and not the stunning views outside. The timber edging around the windows looked to have been sourced from the cove itself, washed up on the tide – and gave the effect of framing the view, much like the pictures themselves.

Most of Tara's work was based around the islands and featured raging seas, calm inviting summer waters and autumnal leaves parting to show a glimpse of the ocean beyond. On plinths all the way along the room were other works, colourful stained-glass pieces, life-like sculptures and beautiful pots. Sam bent to read the inscription in front of one of them and saw that it wasn't Tara's work. He turned to look at her quizzically.

"I've been fortunate enough to be able to set up my own gallery here," she shrugged. "It's only right that I should share my success with others. I give them free space to host their work, giving them some exposure. Look at this one for instance…."

She picked up an intricate necklace which cleverly fused delicate silver strands with stones found on local shores.

"The girl who made this is only 16, can you believe that! Such raw talent. It's a privilege to be able to give her some space here so that she can get the following she deserves."

Tara's big brown eyes blazed with passion. She was incredibly proud of her gallery, chiefly because of what it could contribute to the whole island.

Sam took the necklace from her and studied it carefully.

"It is beautiful," he said, looking across at her and for a moment Tara wasn't sure if he was still talking about the piece of jewellery.

Her breath caught in her throat and her heart beat hard in her chest. Just gazing into those deep blue eyes could get a girl into all sorts of trouble. How easy it would be to just reach out now, to run her fingertips along that chiselled jaw, to feel the softness of his dark hair, to….

The bell over the door jangled and Chris walked in. Sam immediately recognised him as the good-looking man who had been with Tara at the exhibition the night before. His jaw tightened instinctively.

Chris stopped a few steps inside the gallery when he saw the pair standing side by side. Tara stepped back.

'I must look like a guilty schoolgirl,' she thought as Chris looked quizzically from one to the other.

"Everything alright?" he said slowly, not for the first time.

"Yes, yes, everything's fine," replied Tara hastily. "Sam was just admiring Lucy's silverwork."

Sam's heart had sunk when Chris walked in, so he busied himself by looking at the piece of craft, twisting it this way and that in his fingers.

"I'm no expert," he said. "But even I can see that it's stunning. So unusual too. Look, if it helps, I know a jeweller in London. I'd be happy to take some pieces back with me to show her."

Tara was floored. What could she say to that? If the London jeweller liked the work – and she could see no possible reason why she shouldn't be as bowled over as she was – then Lucy could be catapulted into an incredibly successful career. It was too good an opportunity to miss. And yet by doing so, Sam Kerchavel wasn't going to make the quick exit from her life that Tara was hoping for.

"I'm sure she'd be thrilled. I'll get hold of her and tell her."

The two men appeared tense again and it was making her squirm. She needed to get out of there and Lucy's artwork was providing the perfect excuse.

"In fact I might walk up to her house myself and tell her mum, if you're still OK here Annabel?"

There was no suggestion that Sam or Chris should accompany her. Annabel was just returning to the counter, carrying a tray of tea.

"Oh yes of course," she said, oblivious to the tension in

the room. "Yes, you go ahead. Chris can have your tea. I won't get locked into the storeroom again either."

"Good to hear," said Tara.

She suddenly realised that it might come across as a little rude, especially as Sam had just bought *Island Dawn.*

"It's not far, so I won't be very long."

She nodded towards the dog.

"Come on Del, let's go."

The German Shepherd who was lying in her bed by the side of the counter, didn't move.

"Del I said come on, let's go."

Tara walked up to the counter, reached behind it and pulled out a dog lead. The hound immediately sprang to life, jumping up and chasing her tail with excitement.

"I was hoping we could catch up," Sam said hurriedly, concerned he would miss his chance. "Can I walk with you?"

"It's only a few minutes away," Tara said.

She was daft to think that Sam would be diverted and realised she would have to listen to what he had to say at some point. But she planned on using the short walk to and from Lucy's to build up some solid steel defences against him. She knew what Sam Kerchavel was like and she wasn't going to be conned again.

"I'll take over here when I get back," she said flatly. "If the gallery's quiet you can ask me what you want then. If not, you'll have to wait until lunchtime."

"Fine," said Sam, a flash of annoyance crossing his face.

In his world he wasn't used to being kept waiting and he didn't like it. Especially after five long years.

"Come on Del," Tara called the dog and Sam watched her leave.

"Strange," said Annabel who was also watching Tara go, a puzzled frown on her face.

"What is?"

"Why she's suddenly started with that nickname. For the dog – I mean no wonder she didn't realise Tara was talking to her when she was getting her to go for the walk. She's never called her Del before."

"What's her usual name?" Sam asked.

"Delilah," said Annabel.

With which an elderly couple entered the gallery and she bustled across to greet them.

'Whoa,' thought Sam. 'What's that all about? That can't be a coincidence – the question is what does it mean? Tara's German Shepherd dog is called Delilah - and my full name is Samson.'

CHAPTER 7

Frustratingly for Sam, Tara's gallery proved hugely popular for the rest of the day.

Chris was wrapping a couple of prints when she came back, with others waiting to be served. Sam had been hanging about, feeling awkward and spending an inordinate amount of time looking at each piece of art. He decided it was best to duck out of the way but when he came back at lunchtime the place was busier still.

"Sorry," Tara called out as she tapped some numbers into the till. "I can't make lunch."

"But you must stop for something to eat, surely?"

Tara gestured her hand to the rest of the gallery which was now swarming with people.

"Not on days like this. Especially at this point in the season. The visitors will be few and far between soon and so you have to make hay while the sun shines."

She flashed him a wide smile which took his breath away. She always reminded him of the summer, with her golden hair like a halo of sunshine and her happy positive outlook on the world. At least she used to.

"Well dinner then," he said firmly.

It wasn't an invitation, it was an instruction and Tara's eyes narrowed. Then her shoulders slumped a little as she gave in.

"Fine," she said.

"And in the meantime, why don't I do you a favour and pick you up a sandwich? I could take Delilah for a run at the same time. Interesting name for a dog."

Tara's hands flew to her mouth in shock and her eyes widened. Before she could say anything, Sam threw back his head and laughed.

"It wasn't quite the impact I'd hoped to have on you but at least it meant you hadn't forgotten me," he said, reaching for the dog's lead.

For the second time that day, Delilah jumped up with excitement, before following Sam obediently out of the gallery and onto the beach, leaving Tara open-mouthed behind them.

Not for the first time, Sam was stunned by the beauty of the island. He left his bike outside the gallery and instead set off on foot, with Delilah in tow. The dog seemed friendly enough and well-behaved but neither of them was used to each other and so he decided to keep her on the lead. The café was busy too and so he chose to walk away from the village and over to another part of the island. He could pick up a sandwich for them both on the way back.

Delilah trotted happily alongside him.

"Lovely as you are, it's also a strange choice of dog breed," he told her as they walked along the coast path out to the edge of the island.

"If I'd pictured Tara with a dog I'd have said a Labrador, or a cocker spaniel. Or maybe even a dachshund. I wouldn't have thought 'German Shepherd'."

Sam had desperately wanted a dog as a child and his first job at age 11 was setting up a dog walking business, taking the local pooches out for a daily run before and after school. He had those animals to thank for triggering the entrepreneurial spirit in him. He'd done it to help his mother out and would slip her some cash when his father wasn't looking; money that could be spent on food and bills and not wasted on booze or gambling on the horses.

It had proved essential for their survival but the experience of earning his own cash had a dramatic effect on Sam and he was determined to work for himself. It also helped his calling as a property developer, as he visited a huge range of homes each week. He loved the different architecture – the old rambling terraces or the ultra-modern, three-storey homes. He learnt something from every place he visited – décor he loved, décor he hated, the way light spilled naturally into one home, while another was dark and dingy.

He had learnt all this and more from the simple task of taking a dog for a walk. As his business grew he had more and more income at his disposal, yet had never bought his own four-legged companion.

"That's something else that needs to change when I get back," he said aloud. "I need to get myself a dog and a bike. Sounds great. Now how about we just sit here for a bit, take in the view and you can tell me all about your mistress and what she's been up to for the last five years. Oh and what that bloke Chris has to do with it all?"

Delilah whined and nuzzled his hand as Sam sat down on a patch of grass at the top of a small mound of rocks. He stroked the canine's head tenderly.

Ahead was another island and he quickly took his phone out of his pocket to see where it was. St. Martin's, according to Google maps - somewhere else to explore before he headed back to the rat race.

He lay back in the grass with his hands behind his head. Delilah snuggled up next to him and laid her head on her chest. He could see why Tara had chosen her as a companion.

Sam couldn't remember the last time he had been completely alone. With success had come huge swathes of people…assistants, marketing executives, other Directors, accountants, a chauffeur, helicopter pilot, housekeeper, gardeners, construction contractors, you name it, Sam Kerchavel had one. He was blessed he thought, as he lay back looking at the sky. He was blessed to have made a fortune doing a job he loved, with a team beside him who were great too. They might see him as the Boss – in fact lots of people called him just that – but he saw all of them as his equal; they were all in it together. Except one of them seemingly wasn't. Someone was betraying not just *him* but all of the people who worked for Kerchavel Holdings. And he was damned well going to find out who it was.

A small cloud passed across the sun, throwing a shadow across Sam and the sleeping dog.

"How apt," he whispered so as not to wake Delilah who was starting to dream, her legs twitching as she chased some imaginary rabbit, or possibly saw off her mistresses' ex-fiancé in her gallery!

"So Delilah, how come she needed you? You're more than just a fluffy companion to take on walks across the island. There's more to it than that, I can feel it. It seems a little extreme to have some sort of guard dog in a place as beautiful and peaceful as this."

Sam frowned. He had hated it last night when Tara had cut her hand, especially as he felt to blame for startling her. But the thought of something that really worried her, well that was a whole other level of feeling.

"I'll damned well make sure I get to the bottom of all of this tonight," he promised. "Is it tied up with why she left? And if so, how? And what's it got to do with me?"

Sam cast his mind back to their relationship, even though it was something he'd been trying hard not to think about. He'd put all of those memories into a box, sealed it up and dumped it in the furthest recess of his mind. Dragging it out to the surface was painful but seeing her, being close to her was sheer agony, so it couldn't get much worse.

He recalled the first time they met.

"Come to this art showing tonight with me, will you?" his flatmate Malcolm had urged him, that fateful night six years ago.

"An art show? Sorry, I've got a deadline on a new contract to meet, so I'll have to pass."

"There'll be lots of cute girls there."

Sam had looked up from his laptop and raised an eyebrow. Unbeknown to Malcolm he was actually more interested in the art, something he'd learned to appreciate from his mother – as she was a graduate from an art school. Sadly, that was where she'd met his father, but that was a different chapter.

"Girls eh? I guess that's why you're so keen to go."

Malcolm had never shown any interest in anything more creative than the telly but he did have a somewhat unhealthy interest in the opposite sex.

"Maybe I fancy getting myself more cultured. But I need someone to go with. Please?"

"I can't Malc, seriously I need to get this contract finished tonight."

"Just for an hour then. In and out. That's all."

Sam had closed the lid of his laptop in exasperation. It was unlike Malcolm to be so persistent.

"Can't you take Olly? Or Mick? They'll only be heading down the pub otherwise."

"Tried them, they're both tied up."

Malcolm was standing in front of Sam. He was already sporting the only shirt he ever wore out at night, a pale silver number which made his skin seem even more sallow than usual. Sam often wondered if he should tell him, but could never find the right words. It hung from Malcolm like a silvery tent.

"OK, OK," Sam had held his hands up in mock surrender. "But just an hour, yeah?"

Turned out that hour changed Sam's life forever. The event was a graduation showing at the local art college.

"Had I seen one of her works before I spotted her? Or

was it the other way around?" he mused, trying to remember the exact sequence of events.

Delilah, who had no way of knowing, groaned a little and rolled back to sleep.

One thing was for sure, Sam could still remember the breath-taking moment that he first saw her. He was coming away from the bar with a couple of bottles of beer and caught sight of a sheen of silvery blonde hair which seemed to dazzle in the light of the room. She turned slightly, as she talked to a group of (mainly male) interested admirers and he almost choked on his drink.

Tara – Tamara as she was then – was the most beautiful creature he had ever seen. Her glowing, pale skin and the almost imperceptible turn-up at the end of her nose made her look like a wide-eyed, innocent angel. She'd been laughing at something someone had said, her mouth wide and her lips full.

"I want to marry you," Sam had said.

"What did you say, mate?"

Malcolm had caught up with him, took the other beer and followed Sam's gaze.

"Oh er nothing," Sam said hurriedly. "Just talking to myself about how busy it is."

His flatmate would've thought him bonkers if he'd heard him talking about marrying some stranger he'd never even met. Besides, there was always something he'd not quite trusted about Malcolm; a certain slyness about his old school friend who'd suggested they shared a place together in London.

Sam had made an excuse and walked off in the opposite direction, even though he was desperate to go and muscle in on the conversation with the stunning blonde. He'd decided to wait until Malcolm had disappeared and then he'd approach her, try to talk to her.

Sam had never had a problem talking to women. In fact, the problem was often the other way around – trying to keep them at arm's length. It had started to happen when he was about 17 or 18, as he reached his full height of 6ft 3 and his body started to become muscled and hardened. He had his mother to thank for his colouring of dark hair and striking blue eyes and he supposed he should grudgingly thank his father for his chiselled jaw and strong nose. His father had been a handsome man, still was presumably. Unfortunately, he used his looks to hook in innocent women like Sam's mother. He was good-looking on the outside but ugly beneath the surface.

But on this occasion, Sam had had no idea what to say to the angelic beauty who was like a magnet to everyone in the room. Tongue-tied, he had wandered aimlessly around the gallery hoping to catch her attention, without seeming to be hanging on her every word like some sort of loser.

Fortunately, he was soon lost in a piece of art on the walls, which depicted a fast-flowing river, with water dancing in the sunshine. There were two figures on the river bank, who were entwined with their backs to scenery. It was stunning - in some ways a traditional piece and yet the artist had managed to create a completely contemporary twist on the scene.

For a moment Sam had forgotten all about the girl with the golden hair and stood transfixed, drinking in the scene.

"Do you like it?"

He turned to see the very girl standing next to him and he had to fight hard not to turn into a quivering wreck. Up close she was even more beautiful, her large brown eyes questioning.

"Yes, yes I love it. I really do," he had replied honestly. "It's exhilarating. Do you know who the artist is?"

"Me, actually."

Sam was astonished. Beauty and talent all rolled into one person.

"Tell me what you like about it."

He had and from that moment on he and Tamara had been inseparable.

"We spent eight beautiful months together," Sam told the snoozing dog. "And then, hey presto. One day I went to her flat straight from work but she was gone. Taken all her stuff. Not so much as a note. I even called the police."

Delilah opened one eye and gave him a look.

"Yeah you're right, dumb eh? And then five years later I come here for some art exhibition with my mum and bam! Here she is. Oh no - mum!"

Sam had completely forgotten that when he'd left his mother after breakfast he'd promised to join her for dinner that evening. He wondered if Nick had arrived on the island yet, or whether one of her new friends might have invited her instead.

He texted her right away.

Wondered if you have other plans tonight? Don't worry bout me if you have x

Her reply was swift:

No, no other plans. In fact, looking forward to spending some time with you xx

"Great, now what?" Sam asked the dog, as they walked slowly back towards the é.

He desperately wanted to spend time with Tara – on the surface because he wanted to know what had prompted her to leave him in such a devastating way. What he didn't want to admit was that he also just wanted to be near her, to soak up her presence. And yet, his mother had been there for him his whole life and had never let him down. He owed her far more than he owed Tara.

*****

Tara meanwhile was rushed off her feet in the gallery, which was a small mercy. But she found that even as she rang up the till, wrapped pieces in bubble wrap or cardboard, in order to protect them for their onward journey, Sam's handsome face kept springing into her mind.

'And now even Delilah is putty in his hands,' she thought ruefully, as she smiled at the next customer who was queuing at the counter and took their purchases from them.

She wondered what Sam made of the dog's name? She had tried to cover up the fact that her German Shepherd was called Delilah to his full name of Samson. With that as a first name, she knew Sam had always been acutely aware of the Bible story in which Samson lost his strength at the hands of

Delilah. When Tara had been searching for a name for her beloved dog it seemed perfect and she never expected to see her ex-fiancé again. Besides, most islanders thought it had something to do with the large uninhabited island opposite St Mary's, which was also called Samson.

'Great, here we go again,' she thought wearily. 'Another episode of Sam Kerchavel playing havoc with my thoughts and feelings.'

The customers were still swarming around the gallery when Sam and Delilah came back.

"I've got a bit of a snag this evening," he said as he handed her the dog lead and a chicken salad roll. As he did so he brushed against Tara's arm, sending ripples running up and down, so much so that she instinctively rubbed it with her hand. Didn't he feel it too? He certainly didn't show any signs.

"You see my mother is the main art specialist in the family and it was she who organised this trip," he continued. "And because I don't see much of her I'd promised I'd take her to dinner tonight."

Tara studied his face carefully. Was he fobbing her off? His mother was certainly there with him last night and they had been introduced, so it was probably true. The idea of not going to dinner with him was very attractive because she could then avoid having to answer his questions and drag up their miserable past; but she knew that would just be putting off the inevitable.

Then an idea formed in her mind. This could be the solution! She could answer the questions he wanted with his mother there, that way he'd have no chance to get hostile or annoyed.

"OK then," she said.

"OK what?"

"OK, I'll have dinner with you and your mother. See you at 7.30pm."

CHAPTER 8

The green one. That was the one.

Tara slipped the beautiful emerald dress over her head and it slid onto her body, like a second skin. She walked over to the full-length mirror and looked at herself this way and that.

"Is this the right choice? I've never had dinner with a multi-millionaire before, let alone his mother! I'm going to look like Cinderella beside them."

It wasn't that Tara lacked the means to buy herself an expensive dress for dinner, it was just that she had no need of it.

"Jeans, shorts, a bikini and a couple of shirts have done me just fine over the years," she told Delilah. The dog lay on the rug by her bed, watching her closely.

As a result, Tara only had three dresses to choose from. She had worn the scarlet one to the event the previous evening and of the remaining two, the emerald one was the obvious choice. It accentuated her figure but at the same time was classic and elegant. She also loved the feel of the green silk and knew it was important to make the right impression. Lady Rathers had been involved with lots of art charities in the past and had a reputation for turning them into highly successful enterprises; the islanders were keen that she share her expertise with them.

"I'm acting as ambassador for Tresco too," Tara told her pet solemnly.

The German Shepherd put her head on one side, as if questioning whether that was the only reason Tara wanted to make a good impression!

It was almost time to leave and so Tara quickly pinned up her blonde hair, dabbed on lipstick, some light powder, a touch of mascara and…

"Ta-dah!"

She did a curtsey to Delilah who sat up and barked her seal of approval.

Five minutes later Tara was walking along the lane, trying to enjoy the balmy Tresco evening air and not be too nervous. Sam had offered to pick her up and she'd had a hard time persuading him that no, she would rather make her own way to the restaurant.

'I can't trust the man after all,' she thought and truth be told, she wasn't sure she could trust herself either – only in a totally different way. Far better therefore to arrive – and leave - under her own steam.

The restaurant was busy but the way the tables were arranged ensured each party had its own privacy. Sam was seated at the front with by far the best view over the sea. His mother sat beside him and they both stood up as Tara approached. Sam was wearing a dark suit, with an open-necked white shirt, which gave just a hint of the tanned body beneath. Tara swallowed hard.

"How wonderful that you could join us," Sam's mother greeted her with a kiss on the cheek.

They had met briefly the previous evening and tonight Tara was struck once again by the similarity between mother and son. She felt slightly unnerved by it. Were they alike in personality too?

"I thought you might be cross that I was gate-crashing dinner with your son, Lady Rathers."

"Not at all, the more the merrier. And none of that Lady Rathers nonsense, please call me Elizabeth. Now do sit down and tell me how you managed to get Sam to double book himself. It's not like him at all!"

Was Tara imagining it, or was there a twinkle in the other woman's eye?

She had no more time to think about it because their menus were brought to them. Sam asked for her recommendations and soon they were tucking into delicious lobster thermidor. Dessert was almost as beautiful as one of her pieces of art, a delicate elderflower torte, accompanied by champagne macaroons and of course the thick clotted cream for which the region is famous.

The conversation flowed as easily as the crisp white wine and centred almost entirely on her work. She described faithfully how she had spent some of her childhood in rural France, near the sea, before moving to Brighton. The water had always held a spell over her and that was reflected in the works she had created at college and beyond.

"You've done so well in such a short space of time," observed Elizabeth. "Your parents must be incredibly proud."

Tears immediately sprung to Tara's eyes.

Sam was horrified. Tara had never said much about her parents because the pain was too raw but he should've warned his mother not to bring the subject up. He wanted to reach across and take Tara in his arms, stroke her luscious hair, hold her against his chest and tell her that everything was going to be alright but he daren't. She wasn't his to comfort any more.

Chris's face flashed into his mind. Was *he* Tara's partner now, helping her in her gallery, celebrating her successes and yes, holding her when she needed someone to turn to? Jealously raged through his veins and he gritted his jaw, reaching instead into his pocket for a handkerchief which he offered for her tears.

"Oh my dear, I'm so sorry," Elizabeth said, flustered that she had made a gaffe. "I never meant…I mean I never would have said…"

"It's fine, really," Tara dabbed at her eyes with the piece of dark grey silk, which exactly matched Sam's suit.

"You weren't to know. They…they were killed in a car crash, while I was at college. They were together and it was instant, so I have to be thankful for that. It was a long time ago now but sometimes it still catches me."

"Of course it does. And brothers or sisters?"

"No, no-one."

"Poor you. Sam darling, get Tara a gin and tonic. Or better still, a whisky."

Tara protested to Sam that it really wasn't necessary.

Elizabeth, meanwhile, excused herself to visit the bathroom and Tara hoped it wasn't because she was embarrassed.

While she was gone, Tara finished with the handkerchief and passed it back to its owner. For a moment both of them held the delicate fabric together and then Sam entwined his fingers around hers for just a split second, giving them a gentle squeeze of reassurance. Then almost as soon as he had done so, he let go and put the material back in his pocket.

"I'm sorry," he said gently and for a moment Tara thought she might drown in his troubled blue eyes.

"I should've said something before dinner. Should've warned her. It's my fault."

"No, it's not. Besides, as far as your mother's concerned, we only met for the first time last night, am I right? To have suddenly known that fact about me would've seemed odd."

Sam nodded miserably. He should've told his mother all about Tara on their way here; now it felt like he had misled them both.

Tara understood why he hadn't told his mother, after all what would be the point when they were about to go their separate ways again? Even so, it didn't stop her from feeling hurt.

She decided to put her sadness to one side and change the subject. After all, this was likely to be the last conversation she would ever have with Sam Kerchavel.

"Tell me about your company," she said. "I know it's very successful but don't know much more."

Sam's heart skipped a beat - Tara knew something about his business! It had been in the news several times, as had he, but the fact she had taken an interest was a slither of hope, wasn't it?

"I love it," he said earnestly. "We largely try to take disused pieces of land and create something new there; homes, schools, play areas. Our ethos is regeneration, breathing new life into forgotten areas."

His eyes shone as he talked.

"My favourite part is renovating disused buildings. Every one of them has a hidden, individual beauty and it's my job to try to find it and restore it with my team. It's fantastic to see them revived."

"Sounds like you too are creating art," said Tara, enjoying the easy connection between them.

As he told her about some of his favourite projects, Tara could see the passion written all over his face. They were deep in conversation when Elizabeth returned.

"I'm sorry, I seem to have missed something," she said looking from one to the other.

They both turned towards her. She was eying them suspiciously, trying to put the pieces of the puzzle together. They saw the penny drop in her mind.

"Have you two met before? Before last night I mean?"

"Oh yes, yes we have," Tara said with feigned innocence.

Sam could see exactly what Tara was about to say next and knew it was going to spark more questions for him than he could deal with.

Too late.

"We know each other very well," Tara told the older woman. "In fact, a few years ago your son and I were engaged to be married!"

CHAPTER 9

"Well, that was quite an evening," said Sam.

They had accompanied his mother back from the restaurant to her room, shortly after Tara's bombshell. His mother hadn't said too much at the time, not least because she'd spluttered so much on her drink that Sam had had to leap forward and pat her on the back to stop her from choking.

Now they were walking towards Tara's cottage.

'His mother really had no idea at all,' Tara thought, trying to numb the stab of pain.

It had been one thing for Sam to admit that his mother knew nothing about them, quite another to genuinely realise it. It showed her what she already knew, Sam's feelings for her had never run deep. Anyone who was invested in a relationship, was honest and true would have been keen to share the news of their engagement as soon as possible. But someone pretending to be someone they weren't...they'd be sure to keep it a secret.

She tugged her black pashmina more tightly around her.

"You're very quiet," said Sam.

"Uh-huh."

"I think I'll have some explaining to do when I get back."

"So I see."

Tara stopped and turned to face Sam, her eyes glittering with anger.

"I have to say I was surprised that she didn't know *anything* about me at all. It was one thing not to know about the engagement but she didn't even know I existed until last night. But then again, as it was all a big con that was the last thing you wanted – to tell your mum. She might have wanted to meet your bride to be, before you'd had a chance to wriggle out of the relationship. Well, she knows now and if she asks lots of tricky questions, tough luck."

"What are you talking about, a big con? What was a big con?" Sam retorted. "As soon as we got engaged I'd booked us tickets as a surprise to fly to the south of France to tell them ourselves. They lived there at the time and so that's why you hadn't met them sooner. I'd made plans to go and spend some time with them because there was no way I was going to tell my mother and Nick something that important over the phone."

"So you say," Tara snapped.

"So I say? What's that supposed to mean?"

"You know what it means. You were never honest with me, never completely."

Sam was astonished by her words; she was a fine one to talk!

"What are you talking about? I was always honest with you and I *had* planned to take you there. If I'd known you were going to accuse me like this, I'd have kept the tickets as evidence. But of course when I arrived at yours after work I discovered you'd done your midday flit, leaving me high and dry."

"Well, I'm so sorry, take the cost of the tickets off the price of the painting, if a reimbursement is that important to you."

"You know it isn't about the money."

"Isn't it? You just said it was."

Sam was trying to control his temper but the years of heartache and loneliness were making that difficult. For her to suggest that the misery he had endured was anything to do with cash was outrageous.

"Of course it wasn't about the money. It was about the fact that I came home from work, with two tickets to Nice, expecting to surprise my fiancée, only you'd gone. Left. Taken everything you owned. No-one knew where you were. There was no note, no forwarding address, nothing," Sam's voice cracked a little as he remembered standing on the doorstep not understanding the news from her flatmate that she had left, before tearing his own apartment apart in the vain hope that he might find a clue as to her whereabouts.

"Why the hell did you do it Tara? You treated me like dirt."

"You know why. Our relationship was just some big game to you, a joke. Don't give me all that pretend hurt stuff."

Tara started to walk away but he grabbed her wrist.

"Oh no, you don't," he said grimly. "You're not going

anywhere until you tell me what you're talking about."

"Let go of me."

Sam didn't loosen his grip.

"Not until you tell me why. I've waited all these years to know – the least you owe me is an explanation. Put me out of my misery and tell me now."

Sam's words were ragged in his throat. He yanked Tara close to him and her pashmina slid from her shoulders as her body pressed against his. He could feel the heat of her through her dress and his suit, sense the fast beating of her heart. His other hand stroked her long hair, feeling the softness that had haunted his dreams all these years.

"Why do you still do this to me?" he ground out hoarsely, his lips inches from hers.

Tara wanted to resist. Her scrambled brain was screaming at her to push him away, not let him in through her barriers again but her heart was urging her forward. If she just moved half a millimetre their lips would meet and she would be lost.

Her eyes widened as she drank in Sam's piercing blue ones. This wasn't an act was it, the desire, the passion in his eyes? What they were experiencing was a wave of emotions which she thought had long died but like a volcano had just been lying dormant, waiting to be re-awakened.

"Everything was the truth…this was real," Sam murmured and he moved his mouth closer to hers.

Tara closed her eyes in anticipation.

Nothing happened.

She paused another heartbeat, then felt Sam step back, his grip on her wrist loosening.

Her eyes flew open.

"I'm sorry," Sam's face was one of raw desperation. "I'm sorry. I can't. It's not right. I shouldn't, we shouldn't.... damn it!"

He raked his hand through his dark hair distractedly.

"Sam, what is going on?"

"I can't...do this. Not now."

Tara's body stiffened. A few moments ago she had thrown caution to the wind, trusted her instincts and had given in to Sam Kerchavel yet again. Now – what? He couldn't do this? What the hell was that supposed to mean?

"I suppose this is all just another of your games," she said, her voice ice cold.

She bent down and picked her discarded pashmina, wrapping it around her body tightly.

"A game? No Tara, it's not that. I just..."

"Just what? What is it exactly Sam, tell me."

"I can't, I can't tell you now. Just trust me for a few days Tara, will you? Just trust me."

"No," she said flatly. "I've done that before. I can't trust you ever again. I won't."

Just then an older couple rounded the corner and Tara hurried towards them.

"Mr and Mrs Sales, lovely to see you. Sam here was being kind enough to walk me home but as you're heading that way could I go with you instead? Save him the bother?"

"Of course," the couple said, nodding towards Sam.

They were seemingly oblivious to the drama that had just occurred between the couple.

"No, Tara....it's really no trouble," Sam said hurriedly.

He was desperate to explain but what could he tell her?

"Goodbye Sam," she said through gritted teeth.

She made it sound like a final farewell.

Sam watched her walk away with the other couple, her head held high. As she neared the corner, she turned and looked back. Their eyes locked and he almost ran after her because he knew that look but couldn't understand why she should be sporting it.

Because for a moment Tara looked afraid.

"Don't go after her now," he said. "But Sam Kerchavel, somehow you need to get to the bottom of what went on, why she thought for one moment that you didn't love her and what she is scared of."

Not for the first time, he wondered about the time he saw Tara and his flatmate in a café the day before she left. He'd been driving past and almost stopped as they'd seemed to be having words. He'd started to ask her about it over dinner but she was distracted and left early saying she felt unwell. The next day she was gone. Malcolm had always claimed Tara'd been upset over the way he'd treated her friend and given his behaviour, that seemed to fit. But even so, Sam had always wondered if there was more to it.

Once Tara and the couple were out of sight, Sam turned and walked back towards the apartment to face the music with his mother. He was deep in thought, oblivious to the moonlight on the sparkling sea just a few feet away from him.

Why did Tara think he had lied to her in their previous

relationship and what about?

Sam cursed himself for almost kissing her. She had taken his breath away when she had walked into the restaurant in that green dress. He had never met anyone as beautiful as her. Her radiance, the sweetness of her perfume, the closeness of her had overtaken him and he had lost control of his thoughts. If he'd been logical, kept his head, he could have got to the bottom of what had gone on in their past, started to find a way to make amends. As it was, he had blown his chance, maybe forever.

"No, not forever," he said, kicking a stone across the lane with some force. "I'm damn well going to stay on this island until I find out exactly what happened."

Sam was used to having everything under control; he'd built a hugely successful business by doing just that. Yet here he was flummoxed by Tara's words. And she wasn't the only thing in his life that he wasn't sure of – the fact that someone seemed to be slipping trade secrets to this mystery business competitor was troubling him too. To have this business issue and now Tara's assertions that he had deceived her were deeply concerning.

Worse, his near kiss with Tara had brought into sharp focus the other area of his life which needed addressing, something which he had denied for a long time. Now he realised what needed to be done, though he had a sinking feeling sorting that out would be far from easy too.

"They say everything comes along in threes," he muttered grimly. "Especially problems. But now I need to fix them."

CHAPTER 10

Fortune favoured Sam the next day. He had promised to be back for lunch and no doubt more of his mother's forensic questioning but at least she had given him her blessing to explore more of the island for a couple of hours in the morning.

Not surprisingly he had had a restless night. He needed to regroup and work out a plan.

His mother had already started talking about leaving the following afternoon and he sensed that she thought some distance between him and Tara would be a good thing. Besides, he couldn't in all seriousness leave the business for too long, no matter how capable his team. That didn't give him much time.

He also wanted to take the opportunity to go for a swim, enjoy the warmth of the sun on his back, spend a little more time in this welcome solitude. Part of him missed the hustle and bustle of his normal business life but this period away had made him realise how little time he spent on his own. He had already asked Mel to make sure that in the future there were a few gaps in his schedule so that he could get away. She was also sourcing a bike for him - but the puppy he would choose himself.

He had always wanted to explore the highlands of Scotland and taking a dog with him would be just perfect. He'd flown over them in his helicopter a couple of times after business meetings in Aberdeen and his military-trained pilot had swooped down low along the rivers before soaring up over the mountains. It had been one hell of a ride and Sam had fallen in love with the area from the air but until now, he'd done nothing more about going back to visit.

The Isles of Scilly were stunning too but in a different way.

He strolled along the path, past the entrance to the famous Tresco Abbey Gardens and towards Carn Near, one of the slipways where boats landed the many day trippers from St Mary's. Just as he neared the helipad, where he had landed a few days before, who should come down the path but Annabel, Tara's older friend.

She gave a little wave as she came towards him. Sam had liked her as soon as he met her and could see why Tara and she got along so well. He greeted her warmly.

"Annabel, lovely to see you again. Beautiful day for a walk."

"Oh yes, Mr Kerchavel," she said quickly.

"Please, call me Sam."

"Yes…er Sam. I'm actually trying to have a bit of a breather."

"Oh really?"

"Yes, I own a guesthouse at New Grimsby – that's not

too far from where you're staying but I'm looking into extending it. I've had a call with a builder from the mainland today."

"Oh and how did it go?"

Sam was genuinely interested.

"I'm not too sure to be honest Mr Ker…I mean Sam."

"Oh really?"

"Yes. I suppose it's hard when you're just talking on the phone," she said. "But I'm not sure he quite understood what I wanted and I don't think I made myself clear either. So we got into a bit of a fix and it just didn't feel right. It probably sounds rather silly to someone like you."

"Not at all."

Sam had made a career of going with his gut. He had a killer instinct and it had never let him down. But he too knew how Annabel felt; at first it was hard to trust a reaction that was so primeval, so opaque. Now he was comfortable with it.

"Would it help if I took a look?"

Annabel's face brightened for a moment.

"Would you? That would be so helpful. But then…"

Her face fell.

"You're so busy and with lots of important business things to do, I'm sure you don't want to be troubled with something as trivial as this."

"Not at all," Sam said genuinely. "I'd be happy to help. Besides, I'm on a day off."

"Oh goodness even more reason not to show you my place."

"Call it a busman's holiday then," he said taking her arm. "Now, lead the way."

On the way they slipped into easy conversation about the island, its history and current fortunes. Sam desperately wanted to ask about Tara, find out every last thing he could about her, but he thought that might seem too obvious. With a bit of luck he could steer the conversation around to her naturally. And while he was more than happy to help Annabel, if it also helped him get back onto speaking terms with Tara, then it was worth it. A bit of detective work to help him find out what the hell was going on, wouldn't go amiss. He was going to find out what he could about her life here on the island and her friends. Especially the mystery man, Chris.

Annabel's guesthouse was a large imposing stone building which looked like a former manor house. It was situated towards the end of the harbour with spectacular views of the sea towards Bryher. As they reached the front door a group of holiday makers burst out, laden with things for the beach.

Sam was impressed as soon as he stepped over the threshold. With whitewashed walls and nautical-themed ornaments, blue striped curtains and matching cushions adorning a large sofa off the main hallway, Annabel had managed to create a home-from-home feel to the place. He noticed one of Tara's works on the wall, a view of the sea right outside the window. She obviously spent a lot of time there, meaning Annabel was very important to her.

He was ushered into a private front room. It was cosy but

small – because most of the property was devoted to the guests. Annabel pulled out a wooden table which was folded flat behind the sofa. She opened up the leaves and fixed them into place. Sam could see why she stored it where she did, as unfolded it took up much of the room.

Annabel reached up to a shelf and pulled out a file of some sketches and drawings of the property.

"This is what I did, I mean they're just rough ideas…I'm no expert," she said in a rush.

She was obviously feeling embarrassed by her work but she needn't have been. Already Sam could see the makings of some good ideas. She also had a plan of the whole building as it currently stood.

"OK let me have a look," he said, taking the papers from her and smoothing them out on the table.

"Would you like a coffee or tea?"

"Great."

Sam was already distracted by the plans, as Annabel headed off into the kitchen. He didn't notice the sounds of her gathering the mugs and the spoons and other paraphernalia needed for their drinks because he was already engrossed. This is what he loved. This was where the heart of his business lay; much like Tara, he took a blank canvas and tried to create something stunning.

After a few moments he examined the ceiling beams, knocked on the solid walls to assess them and checked the measurements of lengths and heights on the plans. Sam knew exactly what he would do if he owned the place and the thought brought that usual burn of excitement that he felt when he was about to embark on a new project. That feeling had never left him, although his day-to-day work was now increasingly concerned with signing big contracts and profit and loss projections, rather than getting his hands dirty on the projects themselves.

'But this time it's not for you, so you need to come up with a few alternative ideas,' he thought as he moved from one part of the room to the next.

The old mantelpiece above the fire was crammed with family photos. Sam was concentrating and didn't take them in but as he leant across to work out a rough measurement, his shirt caught one of the frames and it almost toppled to the hearth below. It would surely have smashed had Sam's reactions not been as quick as they were and he caught it in his hand.

As he went to put it back in its place he glanced at it and his breath caught in his throat.

It was an old black and white photo of....Tara? He looked more closely. It wasn't Tara at all but someone who looked astonishingly like her. Tall and willowy, her pale hair flowing across her shoulders. Her eyes were a little narrower, nose slightly longer but the wide smile was identical and this woman was another beauty. Without a shadow of a doubt this was a photo of Tara's mother and the friend beside her was a much younger Annabel.

'So the two were friends in the past? Is that why Tara came here?' Sam thought.

He heard footsteps approaching and he hurriedly put the picture back. There would come a time when he could ask about it, he felt sure. But that time wasn't now.

"Do you have some paper and a pen?" Sam asked as Annabel came back in carrying the coffee tray.

He took it from her and set it down. As well as the cafetiere, she had also put out a plate of homemade shortbread.

'The food here is far too delicious,' Sam thought as he took a bite of the buttery biscuit. 'I'm seriously going to have to hit the gym when I get back.'

Suddenly, the thought of his state-of-the-art gym at his home in Windsor seemed a million miles away. Was it really only two days since he was last there? It seemed like another planet compared with this idyllic peaceful getaway that he had stumbled across.

Annabel returned with a large A4 pad and a couple of pens.

Sam put all his thoughts of Tara to one side and got to work.

"Now," he said. "From what I can see you have three main options. The first one is this...."

He started to sketch, only the top of his dark hair visible because he was bent double over the paper, as he repurposed the current building with the first of his visions. It wasn't his favourite idea, he had decided to leave that until last.

"What do you think of this?" he said finally, holding up the paper to show her. "It's a way of really opening up the space."

"That's incredible," said Annabel, genuinely delighted. "I would never have thought of it."

"Wait until you see my other ideas," Sam laughed and got to work again.

They both lost track of time. Their coffee went cold, although Sam was tempted by another of Annabel's homemade lavender shortbread cookies.

They were still throwing ideas back and forth when there was a firm knock on the front door. Whoever it was didn't wait for it to be answered because they heard the door open and close.

"Hey Annabel, only me!"

Tara's voice echoed down the hallway and Sam froze.

"Blimey, you wouldn't believe what happened last night I went out to dinner with Sam Kerchavel and his mum and…oh….it's you!"

Tara stopped dead in her tracks as she entered the room. Only Delilah who was trotting in behind her seemed unperturbed, heading to Annabel and then Sam for some fuss.

Her owner meanwhile, stared from Annabel to Sam and back again.

"What are you doing here?" she asked in a shocked voice which was barely above a whisper.

"Sam's been helping me to decide what to do with the place," Annabel said hurriedly, as if she'd been caught with her hand in the cookie jar.

"I'd had a chat with the builder from the mainland and didn't know what to do and then I bumped into Sam here and he kindly offered to take a look. And his ideas are good Tara," she implored her friend. "They really are quite something."

"Let's see," Tara said with a voice which seemed a little too light.

Sam stepped away from the table to allow her to have a look. He suddenly felt embarrassed, like a schoolboy does when some of his work has been put on show in the school hall. Here was the talented artist Tara looking through his rough sketches. He felt a fraud.

Her hair had been scraped into a high pony tail and he couldn't help but admire the smooth nape of her neck as she studied one sketch and then the next in silence. You could have heard a pin drop in the room, but for the occasional shuffling of the paper.

Finally, she laid the pieces back down on the paper and turned around to face him. Not for the first time he was mesmerised by her huge brown eyes, losing himself in their rich depths.

"Amazing," she said softly, jerking him out of his reverie.

"What?"

"Truly amazing Sam. You've shown a real insight into what makes this place something more than just a guesthouse and managed to capture that whilst giving it a modern twist. Sympathetic to its setting too."

"Well, I'm very glad that someone of your talents feels it's OK," he said, wanting to punch the air with joy, but resisting.

"I do. I really do," she said softly and once again Sam felt the old connection between them return. This is what he had missed. Beyond the obvious fact that he thought she was the most beautiful creature he had ever laid eyes on, Sam had enjoyed meeting Tara on an intellectual level. It was as if their souls had been partners for all eternity, they had slotted so easily together. Their tastes were the same, their sense of humour complimentary and he could only imagine what it would have been like had they fused physically too. He had tried so hard to push away the memories of their intense connection but her words brought it right back to him again. The pain was agony.

"And I for one, am delighted," said Annabel breaking the tension between them. "I think I'm going to go for the third option, what do you both think?"

"It's up to you," Sam and Tara found themselves saying in unison and for the first time in forever, they both laughed.

"It is totally your decision but for the record, option three is my favourite," Tara smiled at her friend.

Sam's heart swelled with pride. He knew it was a good idea to leave the best 'til last.

"It will still need some refinement but I can ask one of my contractors to come and look at it for you, if you would like? I have one in Plymouth who I trust implicitly and I'm sure he'd be glad of the chance to spend a few days here."

"Oh my, that seems too much to ask, I couldn't!" Annabel protested but Sam gently put his hand up to silence her.

"Let him spend a few days here and he will be very happy," he said.

The trio started to work through the details, when they heard the front door open and close again. Delilah barked.

"Annabel, Annabel, come and see this," a voice called from the hallway.

A young woman, in her early twenties burst in.

"Oh hi Tara – and you too."

"Sam, this is Jenny," said Annabel. "She works here at the weekends. Jenny, what on earth is all this about?"

Sam nodded a greeting to the dark-haired woman who barely acknowledged him, such was her wish to spill her news.

"You won't believe what's outside, just off the harbour. It's beautiful. Come and look. Come on!"

The trio duly followed Jenny outside, Delilah trotting at their heels. Sam was racking his brains as to what it could be. He had already learnt that colonies of seals frequented the islands and basking sharks and other species were often to be found here. So it was unlikely to be some sort of unusual sea creature. But if not that, then what?

As he turned the corner along the side of the house all became apparent. While Annabel and Tara gasped with surprise, Sam's heart sank.

There, on the near horizon, was a beautiful large yacht, gleaming and glistening in the afternoon sunshine. Her hull was dark navy, accentuated with highly polished silver finishes and the many portholes hinted at large living quarters within.

The trio of women couldn't see her name from there but Sam knew it well. She was called The Aramat and she belonged to him.

So, given that he owned her and hadn't requested she sail to the islands, the question was, what was she doing here?

A launch was already speeding towards the harbour, a few

feet away from where they were standing. A man, dressed in navy shirt and trousers, deftly pulled the boat alongside the stone wall and brought it to a bobbing halt, before jumping across with a rope to fasten it securely. Then he turned around and offered his hand.

It was taken by a young woman in a sharp white trouser suit, with a shimmering gold shirt underneath. Her dyed blonde hair was tied back in a sharp bun. She wore enough make-up to sink the launch, her false eyelashes fluttering enough to cause a storm.

Sam's heart sank even further.

The woman was teetering about on three-inch white stiletto shoes, which made her passage difficult as she made her way along the uneven stone harbour. She appeared to be making a beeline straight for Sam.

"There you are," she said as she reached him.

More than a foot shorter than him, she reached up to press her hand against his chest possessively.

"I've been trying to get hold of you, have you not received my calls and messages?"

She looked around at her surroundings with disdain.

"I'm not surprised. Don't suppose you can get a signal somewhere like this."

Tara was astonished. Who was this woman who was so familiar with Sam? And whose boat was it in the harbour?

"Anyway, when I couldn't reach you I got it out of your staff where you were, then told them to bring me here on your little dinghy."

She nodded towards the large boat and snorted with

laughter at her own joke. Dinghy indeed; it was a very large, luxurious yacht!

Sam had fallen uncharacteristically silent because this was a scenario he wasn't prepared for. Tara and Annabel were looking at the woman with amazement. The woman must have felt their stares on her because she turned to look at them, jumping back a step when she saw the dog. Her eyes narrowed.

"Are these friends of yours?" she asked Sam.

"Yes, yes they are," he replied firmly, but without looking either Annabel or Tara in the eye.

The woman looked at him for a moment in disbelief. Reluctantly, Sam stepped forward to introduce Tara and Annabel but she got there first, positioning herself in front of him, placing her body as if to protect - or possess - him.

"Donna," she said tightly, holding a perfectly manicured hand out towards them without actually making any effort to reach them. Touching was obviously beneath her.

"Donna Stevens. I'm sure you've heard all about me. I'm Samson's fiancée."

CHAPTER 11

"Uuuggghhh! Sam Kerchavel, why did you have to come back into my life?" Tara shouted furiously as she stormed up the footpath to the top of the island, ready to cross back along the moorland-like landscape to her studio.

Delilah trotted nervously alongside her; she wasn't used to her mistress being so upset.

When the haughty Donna had made her declaration on the harbourside, everyone had stared at her open-mouthed. His fiancée?! Despite her shock, Tara had smiled politely, introduced herself and offered her congratulations, without once glancing at Sam.

"To think we nearly kissed last night!" she now stormed to her dog.

She'd be happy never to clap eyes on Sam again. But had she stolen a glance at him, as they all four stood on the harbourside – and as Annabel had done - she would've seen the stricken look on his face.

"Whose dog is that? Ugh I hate dogs," Donna had said, as Delilah had poked her head out between the legs of Annabel and Tara.

Donna had backed away a few steps, looking as if she might topple into the harbour at any moment.

Delilah had given a quiet low growl. Although she was as soft as butter, she'd seemed to sense the tension in the atmosphere that this new person had created and it made her defensive. Besides, she could always tell when someone didn't like her or her mistress. Donna had taken another unsteady step backwards, right into the body of her fiancé.

"Oh she's mine. She's harmless, but I can take her home if she's upsetting you," Tara'd said quickly. Any excuse to get out of there.

"Yes, I think that would be best," Donna had said rudely, as if speaking to some sort of servant.

She had turned to face Sam and traced a long gold-painted finger nail down his cheek. Tara had pushed down a pang of envy.

"And darling, I'll get one of the crew to go and get your bags. Not really much point in staying on here anymore when I've brought The Aramat," Donna had looked around her as if there was a particularly bad smell under her nose. It had made Tara's blood boil.

"And I really need to shower and freshen up. You can join me if you want to, after all we have a lot of catching up to do."

She'd laughed at this, then reached up and kissed Sam hard on the mouth in some sort of weird show of possession. Tara thought she might throw up at any moment. She had immediately clipped Delilah's lead on, turned and left. Annabel had followed her as far as the guesthouse and she had carried on across the island alone.

Tara kicked a stone into the bracken, as she neared the summit. She was trying not to imagine what Sam and Donna might be up to now, freshening up together in the shower, his raven hair slick with water, the droplets running down his smooth taut skin….

"Aaaghhh," she said to her pet, making Delilah jump again.

Tara immediately crouched down and rubbed her dog's chest.

"Sorry girl, I didn't mean to worry you. But why did he nearly kiss me the other night if he was already engaged to be married? Just another game to him I suppose. Take it while you can."

Even so, Tara had to acknowledge that Sam had pulled away from her at the last minute, just as she felt sure their lips would meet. A shiver of desire ran through her body as her mind revisited that moment; searching his handsome face, the closeness of him, his intoxicating smell, making her want to give herself up to him completely.

"Ugh you IDIOT!" Tara shouted. "Don't even go there with your thoughts. With Sam Kerchavel it's all about bolstering his own ego. He was probably just trying to see if you would still fall for his charms and like a fool you did, hook, line and sinker – again. How humiliating."

She put her hands to her lightly tanned cheeks and could feel the heat rising.

Luckily, there was no-one else around to hear her ravings as she carried on stomping towards home. At the summit, with its 360-degree view of the northern part of the island, she stopped for a moment because its beauty stole her breath away. She never tired of looking at the bracken laden hillside, which reminded her so much of the moorlands of Dartmoor or Bodmin. Only unlike those beautiful wildernesses, here the land dropped away to meet the deep blue sea all around. She loved to look at the archipelago of little rock formations scattered about, with the lovely St Martin's so close. Usually she would look behind her to tiny Bryher with its scattered houses and campsite, but to do so today would mean gazing upon Sam's beautiful yacht and she wasn't prepared to do that.

"I need to put him out of my mind," she said firmly to the dog, as they set off again. Though it wasn't her mind that was the issue but her heart, because that was where Sam was infused.

"He'll be gone in the next day or so and I'll never see him again. He'll go and get married and I'll get back to normal. In a few weeks it'll be as if he was never here."

But deep down Tara knew that as long as Sam walked the same earth as she did, she would never truly recover from him. The thought that he was to marry someone else was devastating. When she had stumbled across him in Annabel's guesthouse at lunchtime, watched the way he generously offered solutions to her friend, her heart had warmed to him. He was like the Sam of old, the man she fell in love with all those years ago and for the first time she began to wonder why she had doubted him.

Now she understood why.

She walked down the pathway which approached the back of Old Grimsby and her heart lifted a little. At least there was no chance of seeing the beautiful yacht that was dominating the view on the other side of the island from here. She let her imagination wonder what it would be like on board, Sam's taste had always been immaculate. It would likely be painted white, to complement its silver fittings. She pictured luxurious blue sofas which would blend so well into the décor and a large, 1960s-style cocktail bar where guests could enjoy the generosity of their host. There would probably be a long dining table too – Sam always enjoyed sharing what he had with friends. Though when they had been engaged he didn't have too much, but his success and his fortune were definitely on the ascent.

"And I think mine might be too now," said Tara firmly as she reached the gallery.

She was always modest about her success, even though her friends and art fans could see it quite clearly. Tara, on the other hand, was always afraid that admitting things were going well would make her good fortune vanish in a puff of smoke.

Even so, as she walked approached the gallery she appreciated it anew. The timber structure blended so well into the landscape, it was as if one was borne of the other, which she supposed in a way was true. It was her home, her sanctuary and it would be again, as soon as Sam Kerchavel left Tresco.

She saw Chris near the entrance, waving goodbye to a couple of visitors. It would seem they had bought one of her works because the man was carrying a large parcel wrapped in brown paper. Tara quickened her pace.

"Another happy customer," Chris announced and he nodded towards the couple who had just passed Tara.

"Gggoood," said Tara, mortified that her voice cracked as she spoke.

"Tara!" he said in a horrified tone. "Whatever's wrong!?"

"Oh Chris, thank goodness for you!"

She fell into his strong arms and started to cry, her breath choked by heavy sobs. Chris stroked her golden hair and whispered soothing words into her ear, as he guided her towards the gallery entrance, followed by a forlorn Delilah.

Just as they reached the doorway, there was a sound of hurried footsteps and Sam came into view. He stopped dead in his tracks as he took in the sight of Tara being held by Chris. Tara could not see him from where she was pressed against Chris's chest and was sobbing so loudly that it was unlikely she could hear him either. But Chris could. The two men's eyes locked. Chris scowled darkly at Sam, daring him to come any closer. Then he led Tara gently into the gallery and closed the door firmly behind him.

*****

Sam tossed and turned all night. As dawn broke he got up and threw on his t-shirt and ripped jeans, before heading out to the beach. He had resisted Donna's pleas to come and stay in the luxury of the yacht. To be fair, he had offered to arrange a room for her where he was staying but she had not appreciated the rustic charm that he found so enchanting.

"What in this dump? I'm not staying here," she'd pouted.

Was she always this much of a snob? Sam wasn't sure if he just hadn't noticed it before, or if she was just getting worse. He had treated her to dinner at the same hotel where he had taken his mother and Tara the previous evening and was mortified that they were given the same table. It had felt all wrong, Donna was huffy and cool with him, critical of both her surroundings and the quality of the food. She clicked her fingers for the attention of the staff, and complained to Sam, even though he found the place as charming as ever and the simplicity of the dishes made them all the more delicious.

Finally, he was able to call Philip and get him to meet them at the harbour with the launch to take her back to The Aramat. Donna kissed him harshly on the mouth again as they parted, in an almost deliberate display for the few holiday makers and locals who were enjoying an evening stroll.

Only when the speedboat disappeared into the darkness had he taken a deep breath. Solitude again. He was beginning to like it, had forgotten what it was like to be on his own. As his success had grown, so had the number of staff he'd needed and his entourage had got bigger and bigger. He hadn't realised until now that it was only when he slept that he got some peace.

"Thank goodness I'm a people person. I have no idea how an entrepreneur who doesn't like others around would fare," he said with a wry smile.

Then there was the other thought that was troubling him. He had tried to put it to one side after Donna had headed back to the yacht, focussing instead on the moonlight on the water, the sound of the waves washing gently against the low harbour wall and the twinkle of the lights from the houses, including Annabel's guesthouse. But it would not go away. It was the knowledge that he was happier when there was a stretch of water between himself and his fiancée.

No wonder sleep eluded him. Eventually, he had given up and as dawn cracked the horizon with soft yellow hues within a pale blue sky, he set out along the lanes. He had forgotten how much being at one with nature soothed his soul. After a while, he discovered a small, pretty cove. The tide was in but on the turn, the waves lapping gently on the sands. Sam ventured down to the water's edge. He was wearing his swimming shorts under his jeans and had brought a towel along too. The last time – indeed the only time - he'd enjoyed a dawn swim was with Tara, on their camping holiday along the south coast. His pulse quickened when he thought back to that time.

'I never wanted it to come to an end and now I know why,' he thought as he entered the water.

'For all my success since then, I'm not sure I've ever truly been that happy.'

He doubted that Tara felt the same way, after all, when he had followed her to her gallery yesterday it was Chris she had turned to - was he the new man in her life?

Although the sea was at its warmest at this time of year, it was still refreshingly cool. This was the Atlantic after all, with the next nearest landmass America and Canada. It seemed strange to think of those great countries that he enjoyed spending so much time in, thousands of miles away across the sea. They would still be in darkness right now, as it was the early hours of the morning there.

Sam dived under a wave and thrust through the water, with powerful strokes. Physical exercise always calmed his mind and he needed it now more than ever. Conscious that although he was a strong swimmer he had no local knowledge of the tides or currents, he didn't go out as far as usual but instead swam parallel to the shore, so that he could reach safety should something unexpected happen. He made his way along the rocky edge of the island, head down in the water, his front crawl strong and fast. He only brought his face out of the salty water for the occasional breath and continued in this way for nearly half an hour.

Suddenly his right arm caught something, or rather someone. He tried to stop but the force of his forward propulsion sent his body barrelling into them.

"Pe-huh. Uggghh!"

He'd obviously collided hard with another swimmer and she was spluttering in the water. For a few moments they were a tangled mess of limbs, like swirling seaweed pulled by a current. Sam could tell the woman was winded and slightly panicked. She grabbed at his body and he felt her hands catch hold of him firmly. Quickly, he flipped over onto his back, allowing her to land on top of him so that his chest could take the weight of her. This had the result of bringing her out of the water and supporting her, so that she could recover her breath. It was only then that he noticed the golden sheen of hair spread partly across his skin, partly in the water, like a magical mermaid. She rubbed the salt from her eyes and then opened them, the water clinging to her dark eyelashes, making them look even longer and more alluring than ever.

"Well good morning, Tara," he said with a grin.

Her big brown eyes widened with shock.

"Sam!" she cried and immediately pushed herself off him, causing Sam to go under the water for a moment, while she spluttered alongside him.

Laughing, he caught her arms firmly and pulled her close to him again.

"Now, now, that's no way to greet your rescuer."

"Rescuer!" Tara said indignantly. "You're not my rescuer! I was happily swimming along and minding my own business until you crashed into me."

"Hey, what can I say?" Sam released his grip on her and splayed his hands wide in mock innocence, whilst treading water. "I didn't expect anyone else to be out at this time of day. Couldn't you sleep either?"

"I slept perfectly well, thank you, why wouldn't I?" retorted Tara, hoping he wouldn't spot the tell-tale dark circles beneath her eyes.

"Oh no reason, no reason."

Tara, who had recovered from her dunking, kicked her legs and started to make her way back towards the shore.

How on earth had she managed to bump into Sam out here, in the middle of nowhere? And end up lying on his gorgeous, firm chest in the process? Her limbs suddenly felt shaky and weak and not because of the collision. Hopefully

Sam would take the hint and swim back to wherever he had come from. Or crawl under a rock someplace.

"Do you come here often?" he suddenly popped up next to her with a grin, water streaming off that gorgeous face.

No such luck that he would buzz off then. Tara ignored him and kept ploughing on towards shore. She heard a splash and then realised that Sam had dived in underneath her. Seconds later he popped up on the other side of her.

'It's like swimming alongside some sort of annoying shark,' she thought crossly to herself.

She was glad that the day was still early and the light still weak. With any luck he wouldn't be able to make out her tear-stained face from the previous night. She swam even harder, although she realised it was pointless to try to outswim him, no matter how good she was.

"So what I really want to know," he said, keeping pace with her. "Is what I did to make you leave me five years ago? 'Cos to be honest Tara, I haven't got a clue."

Oh my goodness, he never gave up!

"What does it matter now?" she snapped back. "No pun intended but it's really rather water under the bridge, isn't it?"

"Ha ha, very funny," he said, clapping his hands together.

Tara frowned. This was hardly a joking matter, he was engaged to someone else for goodness sake! They were approaching shore fast and it couldn't be soon enough.

"I think it's better we let bygones be bygones. We are different people now with *very* different lives."

Tara emphasised the word VERY. She was becoming

incredibly successful but would never reach Sam's level of wealth. Luckily, that had never interested or motivated her and she was more than content with her life on the island. She had everything she needed, or at least would do once Sam Kerchavel got the hell out of her life.

"All the same I would still like to know," he added.

"Why, what's the point? Why are you insisting on dragging up the past and upsetting things?" Tara turned to him and for the first time he saw the anguish in her face. His heart broke and he reached out but she kicked her legs and swam a few paces away from him.

"You have your life. You have a lovely new fiancée, lots of success and all the trappings that go with it. Now you have one of my paintings too for old time's sake. Everything is perfect for you and so be content with that and stop messing around with my life. I was happy until you came along."

She said the last sentence with such force that it was almost as if she had physically struck him. Tara turned and ploughed through the water towards shore. This time Sam didn't follow her and when she reached the sandy beach she turned to see where he was. He was where she had left him, watching her closely – making sure she got safely back? She couldn't be sure that was his reason but as she shielded her eyes with her hand to make him out, she saw him turn and swim back the way he had come.

Tara shivered as she made her way back to her towel and clothes. Life was beginning to stir on the island, she could see movement in the small café at the head of the beach. A dog walker waved a greeting from the lane. Tara towelled herself off before flopping down onto the sand, exhausted. All her strength was spent and not from the physicality of the swim - instead she was emotionally drained. All of the defences she had built up against Sam had been knocked down by him one by one, only for her heart to be smashed to pieces by the arrival of his fiancée, Donna. To have been so close to him physically just a few minutes ago was absolute agony, another blow to her battered heart and she wasn't sure how much more she could take.

"Just a few more hours, maybe a couple of days," she said reassuringly, wrapping her arms around her bare skin. "Just a little while longer and you can put all of this behind you again and recover. He'll be out of your life forever."

Yet as she sat on the beautiful sands, Tara had to admit that was the worst of it. For all his deceit and his lies, for all the heartache, she loved Sam. She had realised that as she had lain awake during the night. She loved him so much that she knew the agony she was going to have to endure as she watched his beautiful yacht set sail from these islands, never to return.

CHAPTER 12

"A funny thing happened last night," Annabel told Tara the next day.

"Oh really?

"Yes, though I expect it's just a coincidence."

"What was it?"

Tara set down the coffee she'd brought through from the little kitchen in the gallery and eyed her friend. Although the older woman was playing it down, she seemed nervous, twisting a button on her cardigan with her fingers.

"It was a phone call. A phone call from a man who said he understood I was looking to renovate the guesthouse and he was willing to put in an offer to buy the place, making it worth my while. But I hadn't told anyone about my thoughts apart from you, Chris and Sam Kerchavel."

"Was it someone who knew the builder from the mainland, you know, the one you'd been talking to?"

"I thought that at first but he knew details, you know. Things that only we three discussed."

She left the thought hanging in mid-air.

Tara frowned. Sam hadn't been totally honest with her

in the past and certainly hadn't revealed he was engaged until his surprise fiancée had turned up on the island. But surely he wouldn't stoop as low as to betray an older woman seeking his help, would he?

"Do you think it was Sam? That he told someone? He promised that he wouldn't," Annabel ventured, as if reading her thoughts.

"I don't know, I hope not. It doesn't seem to fit his image."

Tara didn't dare reveal that she knew a lot more about Sam's character. She hoped there was a reasonable explanation because if it wasn't for her, Sam would have left the island the day after the art exhibition and would never have had a chance to advise Annabel. She felt partly responsible for the leak therefore, even though she had had nothing to do with passing the information on to the other developer.

The two friends were deep in thought for a moment, each nursing their mug of coffee.

"There's one way to find out. Come on," Tara suddenly went to the coat rack and pulled her jacket from the peg.

"Come on what?"

"Come on, let's go and find out. Let's shut up shop and go and ask him."

Annabel looked horrified.

"We can't just ask him if he told someone about my renovation plans!"

"Why not?"

"Well because we're talking about Sam Kerchavel. Top business man, world famous entrepreneur. We can't just arrive on his boat and accuse him of leaking secrets."

Tara shrugged herself into her jacket and started to do up the buttons.

"We aren't going to go and accuse him. We're merely going to tell him what happened and see if he can help us to shed any light on it."

"Oh well, if you put it like that."

"I do put it like that. Come on, Delilah let's go."

They all bundled into Annabel's tiny Fiat and were soon across the other side of the island, pulling into the parking space alongside the guesthouse. As they stepped out of the car they couldn't help but stare at the glorious yacht.

Tara swallowed down the nervousness that suddenly threatened to envelop her. She had to do this for Annabel because her friend had done so much for her.

"Right come on. We'll borrow Chris's boat to get out there, he's at the gym all day and won't mind. In fact he won't even notice it's gone."

With that Tara strode off towards the harbour, with a protesting Annabel trailing in her wake. As they did so a helicopter whirled overhead, quite low, causing the boats in the little harbour to rock and bob. Tara glanced up. It wasn't one of the regular transports to the island and she wondered briefly who it could be. As it moved away to land, she turned her attention to the matter in hand.

Deftly, Tara jumped on board Chris's speedboat which was tied up alongside the wooden jetty.

'To think, I used to think this was flashy,' she thought wryly.

With a heavy sigh she put out her hand to Annabel and helped her on board. Delilah leapt across easily. Tara pulled the cord and the engine roared into life.

"Life jacket," she said, passing an orange one to her friend.

She found another and pulled it over her own head, fastening it firmly. Leaning forward, she slipped the rope to release the boat and they set off towards the superyacht.

"I'm not sure we're really dressed for it," Annabel protested weakly.

"Dressed for what?" Tara shouted over the noise of the engine and the waves.

"Dressed for going on that," Annabel nodded towards their destination out in the deeper water.

"It looks like we should be wearing more than jeans and jumpers."

"Don't worry, we're not going for dinner," Tara laughed in spite of herself.

Annabel's words got her to wondering what it would be like to have dinner on board. The Aramat looked so grand and unlike the man that she knew. Sam had always loved to entertain his family and friends but she'd known him in simpler times when he was as comfortable in some faded old jeans or a pair of board shorts and a t-shirt as he ever was in a dinner jacket, or boardroom suit. When he'd had friends around it was for BBQs in his back garden, where he would take over the cooking of sausages and burgers, bottle of beer in hand. Now his life was very different, his entertaining on a whole new level. As she approached the stunning, sleek yacht, Tara felt the man she had known was lost forever.

'Perhaps what I'd known was all a front too,' she thought ruefully as she slowed the engine before cutting it completely.

The speedboat slid noiselessly next to the buoy which protected the back of the boat. Beside it was a ladder which led up to the main deck. There didn't seem to be anyone around and Tara hoped that Donna wouldn't be there to greet them.

There didn't seem to be any way her German Shepherd could get up there, so she told the dog to stay. Delilah didn't look too pleased but did as she was told.

"Ready?" Tara said to Annabel.

Annabel nodded.

"You go first, though," she added.

Trying to hide her nervousness, Tara put her foot on the first rung of the ladder and began to climb.

If their arrival by boat had gone unnoticed, their appearance on deck certainly could be no surprise, chiefly because Annabel made an incredible amount of noise complaining about the length of the ladder and how slippery it was because it had been cleaned until it gleamed.

"I really don't think I can go much further, Tara," she said when they were halfway up.

"No, no, I think I might be stuck."

"You aren't stuck," Tara said encouragingly. "Just keep your eyes fixed on my deck shoes and take it one rung at the time. Not far to go."

Given the level of commotion, it was no wonder that Sam's face appeared looking down at them, just as Tara reached the top. He was so close he could have kissed her, she thought as she looked up into those baby blue eyes. The thought filled her with a mixture of alarm and exhilaration.

"Ladies, to what do I owe this pleasure?" he said and put out his hand.

Tara chose to ignore it and instead jumped over onto the deck herself. She wanted as little physical contact with Sam Kerchavel as possible. If he noticed, he made no comment, instead leaving his hand there for Annabel to take. She did so gratefully and he helped her on board, where she stood beside Tara.

"Oh wow," said Annabel, gazing around. "This is beautiful."

She was right. The boat was truly stunning and just as Tara had imagined it. The silver rail and highly polished oak floor which both ran along the length of the deck gleamed in the sunlight. There were two large wicker sofas, topped with luxurious feather down white upholstery, with large light blue cushions. Between them was a simple but stunning glass table, with silver strands entwined elegantly around the edges of the glass. On it lay an iPad, a notebook, pen and a tray containing a coffee pot and a large mug.

'Down to earth,' thought Tara. "I expected bone china tea cups."

Not that it mattered to her because this was the first and last time she planned to ever set foot on this boat or anywhere else within a mile of Sam Kerchavel! If it hadn't been for Annabel's mystery phone call, she wouldn't be here now. At least that's what she was trying to tell herself.

"I was just having coffee, can I get you some? Or tea?"

Sam said gesturing towards the mug.

"I'm sorry to say I can't offer you anything nearly as delicious as your lavender shortbread Annabel, but I expect we have some biscuits on board somewhere."

"Oh I'm sorry we should've brought some with us," Annabel giggled nervously. "I can get some sent over later if you would like me to?"

"I'd love that," said Sam. "Though I don't want to put you to any trouble."

"Oh really, it's no trouble at all."

Sam went across to a phone attached to the wall, and asked for more coffee and tea. Tara elbowed Annabel furiously.

"Owww!"

"What was that all about? Offering to send over shortbread?"

"Well, he said he liked mine," Annabel protested. "I was being nice."

"We're not here to swap recipes, we're here to see if he's been selling you down the river, remember," Tara hissed, as Sam headed back to them.

"Everything alright?" he said, looking from one to the other.

He gestured with his hand.

"Please, take a seat, the drinks won't be long."

Tara didn't remember actually agreeing to staying for a coffee but she chose a seat. She could see where Sam had been sitting before their arrival thanks to the iPad and notebook and so sat as far away from there as was humanly possible. Annabel sat next to her, leaving no room for her ex-fiancé to get up close and personal. Good!

If Sam found it strange that Tara was huddled up to the edge of the opposite seat he didn't show it.

Instead he said:

"How can I help? Or is this just a social call? Which would be very welcome of course, but I get the sense there's something you wanted to see me about."

"Well, it's a bit awkward," Annabel said shuffling uncomfortably in her seat.

"Oh really?" Sam sat forward in his chair, intrigued.

"Actually, I'm sure it's nothing, don't worry. Yes, in fact it really doesn't matter and we shouldn't have come and wasted your time."

Tara elbowed Annabel in the ribs again.

"Ow, Tara!"

Sam looked from one to the other and back again.

"Look there obviously is something the matter, so please just say it. Whatever it is I'm sure there's a simple explanation."

"A man called Annabel asking her about renovating the guest house and some of the details he knew about could only have come from our conversation yesterday. I know I haven't told anyone and neither has Annabel, so that only leaves one person…" Tara blurted out.

Given Sam's track record, she was now pretty certain that he was the leak but actually coming out and accusing him was a different thing altogether.

Sam sat further forward in his seat, a deep frown crossing his handsome forehead.

"Are you sure?" he said quietly. "When was this call?"

"Of course she's sure," snapped Tara. "What do you think, she made it up?"

"No, no not at all, of course not," Sam said quickly. "It's just…well it puts a whole different perspective on things."

To their surprise he rubbed his temples anxiously; Tara had never seen him look so distracted.

"And you're sure," he said leaning towards Annabel earnestly. "You're absolutely certain no-one else knew anything about it?"

"I hadn't mentioned it to anyone else, no."

"And the sketches, could they have been seen by anyone – that woman who works for you who we saw there, for instance?"

"No, I stuffed them into the folder as we went out to see what the commotion was about and put the folder into my desk and locked it," with that Annabel reached into her bag, rummaged around for a moment and then held up a small key.

"You see, here it is. And it's the only one."

"You really should get a spare," Tara added and Annabel nodded.

"I know but as it stands this is it."

Before the conversation had an opportunity to go any further, the man they had seen bringing Donna to shore yesterday, opened a door onto the deck. He was carrying a tray containing a tea pot, coffee, milk and cream jugs, cups, saucers and a plate overflowing with every type of biscuit imaginable. As he came towards them Sam got up from his seat and walked over to the silver railing around the edge of the deck, where he stared gloomily out to sea. Tara had to resist an urge to walk over and slip her arm around him. Despite all that had gone on before between them – his previous betrayal and the fact that he hadn't disclosed that he was engaged to be married, she hated to see him looking so troubled. In fact, she hated to see anyone looking troubled, it's just that in Sam Kerchavel's case it was even harder. No matter how she tried, it was impossible to hide the feelings she had for him. The quicker he pulled up the anchor and set sail out of her life, the better.

The man put the tray down in front of them and they thanked him. He nodded and smiled before retreating below decks again.

Tara and Annabel exchanged looks. It would seem from Sam's reaction that the phone call from the developer was linked to him in some way. Had he indeed spilled the beans about the plans and if so, who to? And why was it troubling him so much?

'Either way, he shouldn't be let off the hook for this,' thought Tara crossly. 'Yet again he's let someone down, only this time it's my friend.'

With Sam seemingly caught up with his thoughts, almost oblivious to the fact they were there, Tara took the initiative and poured some coffee for herself and tea for Annabel. The cups were delightful, delicate white bone china, with subtle classic silver edging, the sort of thing she would have bought if this was her boat.

She offered Annabel the plate of biscuits and her friend took one of the luxurious double chocolate ones. Despite his protestations over the lavender shortbread, the array of baked goodies all seemed home-made. They looked tempting but Tara found she had lost her appetite. Instead she sipped her drink and studied Sam from behind.

No-one could deny he was incredibly handsome and he obviously worked out a great deal. His delicate cotton shirt could not hide the strength of the man beneath, with his powerful shoulders and taught muscles rippling beneath the surface. It immediately took her back to their holiday in the campervan, the two of them falling exhausted onto the sand after spending the afternoon surfing, of his passionate kiss, feeling the hardness of the muscles beneath his sun-kissed skin. They had both agreed that they wanted to wait until they were married before they made love but it was a constant battle to resist each other. How easy it would have been to tear the few clothes they were wearing away and to have joined as one, there in the sand dunes. A shiver of desire went through Tara and she quickly sipped more coffee, the heat of the drink a welcome distraction.

'I wish we had made love that time now,' she thought. 'At least I would have the memory of it. At least I would know what it was like to have given myself to him completely.'

She sighed heavily. Now she had to watch as another woman took her place. She knew that deep down she had made the right decision; if she and Sam had been lovers it would have been even harder to see Donna flaunting the fact that she was his fiancée and it was tough enough as it was.

"Do you think he's alright?" Annabel hissed, waking Tara from her reverie.

Tara shrugged.

"I don't know but he can't ignore us forever. He's obviously told someone."

She gave a loud cough. Sam didn't seem to notice, so she did it again.

It did the trick. He seemed to rouse from his thoughts and came back towards them.

"So sorry. I didn't mean to be rude. Annabel," he reached out and took her friend's hands in his.

She looked like she might faint and Tara could hardly blame her. She knew what it was to have Sam Kerchavel's full attention.

"I owe you an apology. I don't know exactly what happened but I did tell someone a little of our conversation yesterday. It was sparse on details but I shouldn't have said anything at all. Believe me when I say I had mentioned it for an entirely different reason," he glanced at Tara when he said this.

"But in doing so it seems to have turned up a truth – rather an ugly one I'm sorry to say."

He let go of Annabel's hands and sighed heavily, then seemed to pick himself up.

"But you have my word that I will make it right, so please put it out of your mind. You have no need to be concerned. I will sort this and to compensate for my lack of judgment, I insist that you allow me to pay for all of the renovations by way of an apology."

Annabel looked aghast.

"Oh no I couldn't..." she started but Sam raised a hand to silence her.

"I absolutely insist."

"But it's thousands of pounds," she continued.

"I'm aware of that, I drew up the plans, if I recall," Sam laughed and the tension was broken.

"Well, it's very generous of you but really…"

"I'm sorry Annabel but I must insist upon it. I will organise it myself and you will know exactly who is coming to do the work and when. You will have my personal number, so that you can be certain everything is genuine and above board."

Annabel was halfway through protesting further when they heard a

Toot! Toot!

The three got up and went over to the rail. Below them the launch that Donna had been on yesterday was coming alongside the boat. On board was Sam's mother and an older, handsome man who was wearing a light grey suit. He waved up at Sam as they approached.

"Nick!"

The delight in Sam's voice was unmistakable. Tara remembered him mentioning his stepfather several times in the past and again during their dinner. The older man had made a deep impression on Sam and had taken him under his wing. In return, Sam had the utmost respect for his mother's new husband. Tara studied his stepfather closely as he came into view. He was tall and trim, with sandy coloured hair, cut short on the sides. She guessed he must be in mid 60s but he could easily have passed for ten years younger. Like Sam's mother, his face was chiefly unlined except for laughter lines around his eyes and mouth. Tara liked the look of him. For the first time she regretted walking out on Sam all those years ago because she would have liked to have known this couple; even if Sam wasn't committed to their relationship, she at least would have had that time to get to know them a little.

A metal walkway with hand rails along the side was lowered to the boat.

'No climbing up a ladder up the back of the boat for them,' thought Tara wryly.

She almost laughed when she thought back to the two of them clambering up the vessel an hour ago.

Sam's mother came on board first.

"Look who's just arrived!" she exclaimed and her husband went forward to embrace his stepson warmly.

"And look, we found a dog!"

Delilah had obviously spotted the walkway and wasn't going to be left out. She raced across to Tara who bent down to give her a hug.

"You were meant to stay," she admonished the dog gently. Delilah responded by licking Tara's chin.

Annabel shuffled a little from foot to foot, obviously feeling like an uninvited guest.

Sam finished greeting his stepfather and turned to her.

"Nick can I introduce you to Annabel, a new friend of mine."

Nick put out his hand and shook Annabel's warmly.

"And this, this is Tara."

Was it Tara's imagination or did Nick and Sam's mother

exchange a knowing look? She supposed Elizabeth could hardly have been expected to keep news of the previous engagement from her own husband. Tara stood up from cuddling her dog and Nick grasped her hand warmly between his.

"Delighted to meet you Tara."

He gave her a broad smile and Tara found herself warming to him immediately.

"And who's this?"

"Delilah."

Tara let the name sink in for a moment and sure enough, Sam's mother and her husband looked at each other in astonishment. It would not be lost on them that Tara's dog was called Delilah and Sam's full name was Samson.

"Darling, Tara is the talented artist we've all been raving about," said Elizabeth hurriedly to her husband.

"Tara, Annabel, we have to go to our cabins and freshen up, will you still be here later? I do so want Nick to get to know you."

"Unfortunately not, I think we've concluded what we came for."

Tara glanced at Sam. Was it her imagination, or did a look of disappointment cross his face?

"We don't wish to intrude on your family time," she added quickly, so as not to seem rude. "Besides, I'm sure Donna will be pleased to know you've arrived."

"Donna!?" Nick looked astonished and turned to Sam. "Donna's here? On the island?"

"Yes, she is," said Sam coolly. "She's actually down below, in her cabin."

The news that his fiancée was on the boat with them shook Tara to the core. Of course it made absolute sense that having come all this way, Donna would want to be near him but the thought of her being in her cabin – their cabin – just a few feet below, both stunned Tara and filled her with misery in equal measure.

"In that case I need to have a word with you Sam as soon as possible and in private," Nick was saying in a low, urgent voice. "Tara, I must apologise – I would very much like to hear more about your art. Perhaps Lily and I could come and visit you at your gallery?"

"Of course," Tara was touched by the way Nick used his pet name for his wife.

"We should get going really," said Annabel brightly. "I have some guests arriving later and I must get their rooms ready. Sam, thank you for your offer but it really is too generous. Whatever happened, I'm sure it was just a misunderstanding."

"That's one word for it," Sam almost growled, taking his guests by surprise.

Then he brightened.

"Annabel, I really won't take no for an answer. I will have one of my team draw up an agreement for you, ensuring that you have full control over the project but the cost falls to me."

There seemed to be no arguing with the man. Annabel spluttered her thanks and then raced forward and gave him a hug. Surprised but laughing, he hugged her back.

"I wish all of my investments had that sort of reaction," he said.

'And I'm glad they don't,' thought Tara.

The journey back to harbour was short but Annabel was full of praise for Sam.

"Such a lovely man, what a gentleman."

Tara nodded but said nothing. A little way back to shore she turned and looked back. Sam was leaning against the railing of The Aramat watching her, but she couldn't quite make out what the look on his face meant. Sadness? Longing? Regret? Her eyes lingered for a moment longer before she turned to the matter in hand, navigating Chris's speedboat safely back to shore.

When she glanced back again Sam was already deep in conversation with Nick and whatever they were talking about looked deadly serious.

CHAPTER 13

Sam could hardly take in what his stepfather was telling him. He looked from him to his mother and back.

"Nick, can you repeat that?"

"Of course," Nick said kindly.

He knew the news he was delivering to Sam was a deep blow, although his wife secretly thought it was not going to be quite as deep a blow as Nick might imagine.

"You were wondering, no doubt, why I didn't accompany your mother here and why I've been absent for a few days."

Sam nodded. It was certainly true that since Nick had fallen totally in love with his mother, he hated to be apart from her, even for a couple of days.

"It's certainly not something I do lightly, unless it's a matter of great importance."

Nick looked across at his wife and smiled. She was sitting tall and elegant on the edge of the white sofa, watching the two men in her life intently. Nick and his stepson were leaning against the nearby rail.

"I've actually not been too far away these past few days. I've been in Newquay."

Sam was surprised.

"Newquay? As in Newquay, Cornwall? Just a few miles away, on the mainland?"

"Yes. That's right. When you told your mother and me a few weeks ago that a developer seemed to be getting to your deals first, we smelt a rat. As I'm sure you did too. I know you've been incredibly busy, with that deal in Dubai and the forthcoming trip to Berlin, so you had no time to investigate. So we decided to do that for you instead."

Nick stood up even straighter, as if making an announcement.

"And the long and short of it is - we think we have discovered the leak."

"Whoa, whoa, whoa, back up a little bit," Sam said, looking from one to the other.

"You two investigated who the mole was? Was that wise? We're potentially talking a lot of money here and that can drive people to do bad things. It could have been dangerous!"

"Why do you think we kept it from you?"

They all knew precisely why; Sam would never have allowed it had he known.

"But there's no harm done and I went to Newquay alone. Partly to ensure Lily's safety and also because I needed you out of the picture – in the nicest possible sense," said Nick, with a twinkle in his eye.

"Unfortunately, the same can't be said for what we discovered, or rather who. That person was very much in the picture."

Sam knew that Nick was doing him a great favour in uncovering the person who was selling his business secrets but he did seem to be dragging things out a little. Nick liked to have an audience and a drama and was making the most of this one. Sam just wished he would cut to the chase and tell him what he knew. The suspense was killing him.

"The only way was to go to Newquay myself. That was the freshest lead, if you like. It was fairly straightforward to find who the seller was and then I did a bit of undercover work, found out what his interests were and his hobbies."

"His hobbies?"

"Yes, so that I could meet him on his home turf. A chance encounter at the tennis courts, bit of chat over some lunch accompanied by quite a lot of alcohol on his side, and hey presto! He spilt the beans."

Sam was astonished. Nick was an incredible businessman in his own right and had taught Sam the tricks of the trade but he had never imagined him to be this crafty.

"Well, Hercule Poirot, I'm going to have to watch what I do in the future, if these are the sort of tactics you employ!" he joked. "But I am seriously impressed."

"Oh that was just the start," said Nick waving his hand around airily.

"Lily and Mel need to take the rest of the credit. We knew the name of the person who had approached him and I even managed to wheedle out a company name but they were false, of course."

Of course, thought Sam. While so far the deals which had gone to the wall had been fairly small, he felt sure that whoever was doing this would become increasingly emboldened and the financial stakes would get a lot higher.

Which would make the whole situation far more dangerous.

Suddenly Tara flashed into his mind and he pictured her arranging some of her work and that of others on the island in her simple, elegant gallery. In a way Sam envied her. While they were both doing something they loved, his success had been so stellar that it had brought him incredible wealth and therefore a lot of envy. So while he trusted – rather had trusted – his inner circle completely, that was as far as it went. And he trusted Tara too, he suddenly realised.

He allowed himself a moment to picture her dazzling wide smile. She really was the most beautiful woman he had ever come across and he wasn't just talking about her looks. Her generosity to her friends and kindness to others on the island was there for all to see. A pang of pain shot through him. He so would have liked to be sharing his life with her. Quickly, he turned his attention back to his parents, so as to dampen the feelings of sadness.

"Lily and Mel set about searching for this company and any links to you. There was very little to go on online but the few snippets of information I'd gleaned helped a little."

"It was a bit of a needle in a haystack," said his mother, picking up the story. "And then Mel, the clever girl, managed to find just one Facebook post which told us all we wanted to know. I don't know how she did it to be honest, but one thing led to another. They had been very careful to cover their tracks and so it all came down to that one photo in the end. A photo of a party, which seemed innocuous enough until you looked closer, looked at the background…and there was the mole, back to the camera but still unmistakable."

Now his mother was being as dramatic as her husband and was dragging the whole saga out. Sam was itching to know who it was.

"Who was it," he pleaded. "Tell me, who did you find?"

With that the door to the deck burst open.

"Oh Nick, you're here!" cried Donna. "How lovely to see you!"

She was wearing four-inch high espadrille wedges and a tiny purple mini-dress. Sam wondered that she could even walk, let alone race over and give her future father-in-law an embrace.

The atmosphere on the deck was palpable. Sam was desperate to discover what it was his parents had found out but they would have to wait until they were alone again, not least because he had his own details to add to the mix, following Annabel's mysterious phone call. If they tallied, well…

The tension hung around them all like a heavy fog but Donna either didn't, or refused, to notice.

"I had a devil of a job to get here," Donna said. "I knew how pleased Sam would be if I popped over and surprised him but I was never going to be able to get the yacht's number from Mel. Let's just say I thought of a genius way of distracting her and getting the number from her desk."

She laughed heartily at this, the high-pitched sound suddenly grating on Sam's nerves. And she'd tricked Mel? His PA would be mortified.

"I think poor Mel deserves better treatment than that," his mother said evenly.

Sam glanced across at her. She was eying her future daughter-in-law coolly.

"Anyway," said Donna, ignoring the remark. "Once I had the number it was plain sailing. Get it - *plain sailing*! I just pulled rank on that stupid Philip guy - really Sam I think we should consider a replacement. He talked about needing 'authorisation' and I said: 'I am the authorisation! I'm soon to be Mrs Kerchavel, that's all the authorisation you need!'"

Sam could hardly bear to listen to Donna anymore. He would be seeking Philip out as soon as this conversation was over, to reassure him that he understood the position he had been faced with. He would also have to have words with Donna about her behaviour. His heart felt as heavy as lead.

"Anyway, eventually he gave in and so here I am!"

She threw her arms out wide and then tottered over and pulled Sam harshly into an embrace. He thought of the soft, warmth of Tara when they had nearly kissed the other day. It had been like touching velvet and was very different from this experience. This was more like embracing a piece of stone.

Underneath, Sam was seething too, although he wouldn't dream of showing that in front of his parents, let alone other members of the crew. Philip was a good person, who had been with him for three years and was a complete professional. To have put him in this position was unforgivable. There would need to be a conversation with Mel too.

After chattering non-stop for several minutes, Donna stopped and looked at them all.

"Oh, I nearly forgot. I've invited a friend to stay for a

couple of days. Someone you haven't seen in quite a while Sammy. I thought it would be a lovely treat for you. I've told him he'd better be quick though because we're setting sail for home anytime now. He should be here very soon."

Sam's heart sank. He had a horrible feeling he knew who the person was that Donna had invited and if he was right, it didn't spell good news.

CHAPTER 14

Malcolm stepped aboard The Aramat and took in his surroundings. He'd never been on board before and she was magnificent, everything he'd imagined and more! Donna had done an incredible job of landing Sam Kerchavel. He and his former flatmate had been thick as thieves at school and college but that cow Tamara had driven a wedge between them. Even after she had left - done the bunk that she had assured him she would - a coolness had settled between the two men. There was no way that Sam could have known what went on between him and Tamara, Malcolm was sure of that but even so, something imperceptible had shifted and nothing he had done improved things.

It irked Malcolm. He had spent years cultivating this friendship and then that woman came along and derailed his plan.

Thank goodness for his ambitious young cousin, who was also interested in a career in property development. Malcolm had always been her helpful 'Uncle' and he knew that once she'd got her eye on Sam she wouldn't stop until she had landed him. How right he had been. All he'd had to do was make the introduction and leave the rest to her.

"Uncle Malcolm!" Donna squealed as she clopped across the deck to greet him.

Sam felt sick to the stomach. He'd had a feeling his slippery former friend was the guest Donna was talking about but he got up politely and shook hands with her cousin.

"Malcolm."

"Sam."

Sam studied the shorter man's face. There was something about him that didn't ring true. His gut feelings had never let him down before. Not for the first time Sam regretted the fact that Donna and Malcolm were related, he would have preferred not to have seen him again. But to be fair he'd rarely been in their lives since that evening just over a year ago when he had first met Donna (something Sam had since suspected was engineered). Perhaps he could tolerate the odd brief visit.

Sam offered his guest refreshments and passed a polite half-hour with the pair before making excuses to leave.

"I have one or two urgent things to discuss with Philip and a couple of business calls to make," he said, standing up. The former was certainly true. He had to make amends with the captain after Donna's appalling behaviour and it had to be done before Philip took a job elsewhere. As for the latter, well he was still anxious to know what Nick, Mel and his mother had uncovered and to share his own suspicions.

"Oh babe can't you stay a little longer? I've hardly seen you since I arrived," Donna pouted like a small child.

Sam forced a smile.

"I would love to really, but these matters can't wait. But we can catch up later – for dinner? Besides, I'm sure you two have plenty to talk about."

"Oh yes we certainly do," said Malcolm.

Sam didn't quite like his tone and quickly left the deck, glad to be away from them. When Nick had arrived and met Tara on this very deck, Sam had imagined having dinner with the two of them and his mother; a happy family affair. How stupid was that! He already had a fiancée and now Malcolm in tow to boot.

Quickly he sought out Philip and spent some time reassuring him that he'd had no other option but to do Donna's bidding.

"Please accept my apology, had I known about it this would not have happened," he said earnestly. "Rest assured you will not be put in that position again."

Fortunately, Philip was a decent man who knew his employer was being serious and accepted his word. The pair shook hands and parted ways.

Next there was the call to his assistant, Mel. She had plenty to say on the subject of his fiancée.

"She rushed into the office and told me that someone on the floor below had had an accident. Being a first aider, I went immediately, Sam. I should've guessed it was a ruse. She must have rooted around my desk while I was away and got Philip's number. When I got back after realising it was a false alarm, she'd gone. I should've told you right away but at the time I thought it was an innocent mistake on her part."

Sam reassured her, just as he had Philip. The whole thing

made him so angry. It was bad enough that he had a mole in the company that he needed to root out and that he'd still not had the opportunity to hear what his parents and Mel had discovered. All because he was having to sort out this mess that Donna had created because she'd been sneaking around being rude and arrogant.

'Tara would never have behaved like that,' Sam thought.

A sudden realisation struck him as surely as if it had been a physical blow.

That was it!

That was the real reason for his anger, the seething frustration beneath his skin. He was engaged to the wrong person, to someone who could never make him happy, never make him complete.

Meanwhile, the right person thought he was a complete loser and would probably never want anything to do with him again.

"What an idiot you are," he groaned, running his hands through his jet black hair.

"You should never have taken up with Donna. So now you've landed in a right mess and the question is: what on earth are you going to do about it?"

He headed up to the deck, only to discover that the launch had gone. Donna and Malcolm had too – no doubt heading to shore for a visit. He looked over the side and could see the boat heading back towards The Aramat with Phillip at the wheel, cutting through the light seas around the harbour. Sam drummed his fingers on the rail impatiently.

"Come on, come on," he willed the boat to arrive as soon

as possible. "Can't you see that the next few hours could totally change my life?"

*****

Tara was in her gallery, distracted by her thoughts.

Usually she would take the opportunity of a quiet spell to sketch out some new ideas, re-order the packaging needed to transport her paintings to their forever homes, or do a bit of a stock take.

Not today. Instead, her head was racing with thoughts of Sam. Worse, her arms still ached from swimming away from him as fast as she could, another unwelcome reminder.

'How dare he! How dare he tease me that way, when he's about to go off and marry someone else!' she raged.

The bell above the door rang to herald the arrival of some visitors and she immediately slapped on a welcoming smile. The warm September sun was shining, meaning most holidaymakers were outside on the beaches, in the gardens, or walking the coast path but that was fine with Tara. She wasn't in the mood to make polite conversation.

The couple spent a while browsing, then came to the counter and bought a small, original painting and some cards.

Once they were on their way Tara was more than happy to flop down in her chair with a cup of tea and Delilah by her side.

She picked up her book which she rarely had a chance to read and was so engrossed in it that she didn't notice the tinkle of the bell again. It was the rare sound of Delilah's low growl which brought her to her senses and she looked up.

"Oh. Donna!"

Sam Kerchavel's fiancée was standing in front of the counter. Tara wasn't sure if it was the way she seemed to be almost bearing down on her which had alarmed her dog, or whether Delilah remembered meeting her before.

"I thought I might find you here," Donna said coolly.

She was wearing a purple minidress which seemed more like a handkerchief, it was so short. Tara wondered at Sam. His mother was so elegant and he was too; the way Donna dressed didn't seem like him at all. Still, it was personality that mattered in a relationship, not looks.

"What can I do for you?"

Donna traced a long, gold fingernail along the counter and then began to saunter around the room, as best she could in oversized sandals.

"I noticed when I was on the yacht this morning that a large picture had been put up in the lounge, without *my* permission," she said. "When I asked the staff about it they told me it was one of yours and that Sam had been very particular about where it was put."

Despite the unpleasant tone of his fiancée, Tara glowed inside. Sam had put *Island Dawn* up in his yacht in what sounded to be a very prominent place!

"OK. Well Sam's able to buy whatever he chooses and put it where he likes. I'm not sure what that has to do with me?"

"Yeah, right," the other woman tossed her head in disbelief.

"I think you know exactly what it has to do with you.

You see this new painting made me curious, so I did a bit of asking around about you. Didn't take long to find out that you were once Sam's fiancée too."

"With emphasis on the 'were'," Tara said.

She was trying to keep her voice as level as possible. Donna said it hadn't taken long to find out that she had been engaged to him but how was that possible? None of her friends knew of it. If Sam had told her, wouldn't she have just come out and said it?

Trying to appear calmer than she felt, Tara stood up from her chair and placed her bookmark into her novel before putting it back under the counter. She was pleased to discover that she was taller than Donna, which she hadn't realised when they had first met on the sloping harbour slipway, with the other woman wearing ridiculous heels.

"But you're right, Sam doesn't have anything to do with you anymore," Donna looked around her with a look of disgust on her face.

"However, I thought a visit to this dingy little place might ensure we have an understanding."

"I'm listening," said Tara, her body tense.

"I want you to agree to not see Sam again."

A part of Tara thought she could think of nothing better than to see the back of Mr Kerchavel and all the trouble he had caused her but she wasn't going to give this woman the satisfaction of saying so. Who did she think she was, marching into her gallery on the island she called home and making demands!?

"Well I'll do my best, believe me, but it's a small island. I can't guarantee anything."

"Oh I shouldn't worry, we'll be setting sail first thing in the morning," Donna said dismissively and Tara felt a stab of pain in her heart.

Sam would be sailing away from here in less than 24 hours.

"I mean that I want you to promise not to see him again after we've left. I'm sure re-acquainting yourself with a multi-millionaire is very tempting for a struggling artist and believe me I'm used to all sorts of women throwing themselves at him. But he's mine, we're getting married very soon and I won't be responsible for my actions if you try to get between us."

Tara had to admit she was flattered that Donna felt sufficiently threatened to have travelled across the island to warn her off but she was seething too. Delilah seemed to sense it because she uttered another quiet, low growl.

"How dare you come in here and speak to me like that," Tara said in a low voice. "I will see or speak to whomsoever I choose. I didn't ask Sam to come here and it was his choice and his choice alone to buy my most expensive painting."

She let that thought settle on the other woman for a moment.

"But if you must know, we are ancient history and have nothing more to discuss. I am very successful in my own right and so neither need, nor want anything from him."

The last sentence wasn't strictly true – she wanted Sam so badly that she ached for him. But he was betrothed to another and that was that. End of story. Life would carry on and eventually she would get over her heartbreak and get back to normal.

Her answer seemed to satisfy Donna and she saw her relax a little.

"Good," she said, in a hard, bitter voice. "I'm glad we've seen eye to eye. Just make sure you keep it that way."

With that, Donna turned and deliberately bumped into one of the stands in the middle of the room, sending a beautiful glazed vase crashing to the floor, where it smashed into smithereens.

"Oh, silly me!" she laughed harshly and flounced out of the door, slamming it shut behind her.

Tara stood for a few moments with her hands on the counter to steady herself, her breathing heavy. She hadn't been threatened like that since Sam was last in her life and she was shaken.

After a while she fetched a dustpan and brush and began to sweep up the broken vase. It had been beautiful and she was upset to see it in pieces all over the floor. She would have to pay the artist the £200 asking price too, as it had happened in her gallery.

Ruefully, she thought about the last time she was sweeping up something which had broken; the champagne glass that she'd dropped on the night of the art exhibition, when Sam had startled her.

"Why do you always bring such trouble into my life, Sam Kerchavel?" she muttered furiously as she swept up the mess.

"I'm not going to be cowed by a bully like Donna but I'm more than happy not to see you ever again. No matter how handsome or charming you are."

She knew Elizabeth, Sam's mother, had been in

discussion with the islanders about being a patron of their small arts charity and she hoped that wouldn't mean she'd be bringing her son back for future visits. That was at least one of the benefits of her success – Tara could just refuse any invitations that involved Sam. She would be more than happy to meet with Elizabeth, having warmed to her immediately but they could keep their conversations strictly to art and the charity's affairs.

"That arrangement will suit me just fine," she told Delilah who had been sent to her bed away from the danger of the broken glass.

"Besides, he's never been totally honest with me. I've been in love with a dream, an ideal; someone who doesn't really exist."

She thought of the way Donna had sauntered around the room in an arrogant, self-entitled way. Cheek of the woman!

"You know what Delilah, I think they deserve each other. Let's hope Donna is right and they really do set sail in the morning."

Tara looked at the time on her phone.

"If she is, that means there's just a few hours to go before Sam Kerchavel will be out of my life once and for all. And it can't be a moment too soon."

CHAPTER 15

Sam had to ensure that he wasn't going to bump into Donna, or worse, Malcolm, so as soon as he reached the little slipway, he had called Donna, to enquire casually as to her plans. He had been astonished to hear that she was planning to look around the island that previously she seemed to think was beneath her. And no, she didn't want him to accompany her. He hadn't actually offered to go with her but either way, Sam was relieved.

"Is Malcolm exploring with you?"

"For some of the time and then he has some things of his own to do."

Things of his own to do? On Tresco? The old suspicions about Malcolm surfaced but Sam put them to one side. What damage could his old college mate really do in such an idyllic place and in such a short space of time? It probably meant that he had to make some calls, or login and do some work. Besides, as long as he wasn't hanging around with him, that was the main thing. The less he saw of them the better.

Satisfied the coast was clear, Sam ended the call and immediately rang his mother.

Half an hour later and she and Nick were down by the harbour to meet him and head back to The Aramat. Sam was keen to remain on the island, conscious that his time on Tresco was now short but his luxury yacht would give them privacy. It also had the advantage of acting as an early warning system should Malcolm and Donna return early, because they would have to herald the launch to bring them back on board.

The trio had lunch, which Todd the chef had masterfully concocted from fresh seafood and ingredients from the islands.

During the meal they steered away from the conversation that Sam was desperate to have, instead Elizabeth regaled them with her conversations about the patronage of the new charity and the plans the islanders had.

Afterwards, they moved inside to the luxurious lounge and spent a few moments admiring Tara's oil painting, *Island Dawn*, resplendent in its new home. Sam's mother then sank into one of the two large sofas but her son sat forwards, tense and alert.

"Donna. Donna was the woman in the back of the photo. She was at the party with the man who has been contacting your potential business associates," Nick told him gently. "Donna has been betraying you."

Sam felt a little queasy at the news but he wasn't surprised. It had all fitted into place when Annabel and Tara had come to see him to report the mystery caller, who had asked about renovations and whether the business was for sale. He quickly explained this to Nick and his mother.

"I had to come up with a reason as to why I'd stayed on Tresco for so long when there were deals to be struck and money to be made back in London," he explained earnestly. "I've had a lot to think through here and until I reached my conclusions, I didn't want to hurt her. So I'd said something to appease her, which was also partly true - that I'd accompanied Mum to the art exhibition and while I was on the island, was looking into a little renovation project which could lead to bigger things. I told her the name of the place because we were on the deck and I pointed it out to her. I thought it was odd that she was insistent on knowing the guesthouse was called and wanting some of the details."

He rubbed his hands on the top of his knees agitatedly.

"She must have presumed that I'd told Mel and you two and the rest of our inner circle. But this was a favour for Annabel and not part of the business. I wasn't going to be a long-term investor and so I hadn't told anyone, not least because I'd given Annabel my word that it would remain confidential."

Sam kicked himself for telling Donna. He normally wouldn't breathe a word about anything deemed confidential but he hadn't wanted to hurt Donna's feelings and so had revealed too much information. It had never occurred to him that she could be the mole, although at least she was finally unmasked.

"Once we found that photo and spotted her in it we were able to do a little more digging, darling," his mother continued, reaching across to squeeze his hand.

"Nick hired a private investigator and he came back with

some interesting information within 24 hours."

Sam's jaw dropped open.

"You hired a detective?"

"We wanted to be sure. She's your fiancée, Sam, we couldn't accuse her of something if she hadn't done it – that wouldn't be fair. So we went to the best in the business, Tom Reynolds."

Sam whistled. Everyone had heard of Tom Reynolds; he was good but he doubted he came cheap. He stood up and walked the length of the long lounge, agitatedly. He couldn't believe that Donna had caused so much trouble.

Nick meanwhile had reached into his blazer pocket and pulled out a manila envelope, which he placed on the long silver and glass coffee table.

"The report from Tom's team is all here. Or enough anyway. There could have been more information but we pulled him off once he had established the main facts."

"Tell me," said Sam. "Tell me the main points. I'll read the details later."

At this precise moment he wasn't sure that he would ever want to read the details. While he had never loved Donna, he had been fond of her and had been prepared to share his life with her – at least in the beginning. Recently, he had begun to think what a disaster it would be, especially if they had a family together. He'd been nursing those thoughts before he ever set foot on Tresco but seeing Tara again and witnessing the stark contrast between the two women had only cemented his doubts still further. Donna was chalk to Tara's cheese and not in a complementary way.

"It would seem that the man in the Facebook photo is her husband."

Sam gasped and stared at his stepfather in utter disbelief. He thought perhaps this man was a friend, distant relative, or possibly even a lover – but her husband?

"You're kidding!?"

"Afraid not."

"When, how long…? I mean was she married when we first met?"

"Er, just afterwards it would seem," Nick looked faintly embarrassed even though the deception was not his to own.

Sam racked his brains.

"Come to think of it, there was a spell…last October I think, when she said she was staying with an old friend in Greece for a week. I didn't think anything of it, though it was odd that she didn't text or call me. I assumed she was having a nice time."

"A very nice time by all accounts," his mother said sharply.

Sam looked across and saw the anger written all over her face. She would not take kindly to anyone trying to deceive her only child.

"Wow, married," Sam breathed in disbelief.

"I'm so sorry darling," his mother said with a softer tone. "It must be devastating for you but I hope in time you'll see it was for the best to find out now, before your wedding."

"Do you think she would have gone through with it? Marrying me I mean?"

Nick shrugged.

"Who knows? You'd like to think not but to have returned to you soon after her marriage, presumably with the full knowledge of her husband, beggars belief."

The three of them fell silent for a moment, contemplating the sheer audacity of the deception.

"It's a relief really," Sam said finally.

His mother and Nick looked at him expectantly.

"We are worlds apart. We rushed into things. I was distracted by work, she was very keen to push things along. It seemed easy and simple but it was a huge decision and it was the wrong one. I've been feeling terrible about it recently, wondering if I should stick to my word and go ahead with it, which would probably make us both miserable, or end it and risk hurting her. And all along this...."

Sam waved the manila envelope. He really couldn't begin to comprehend it all.

"But could it really have led to bigamy?"

Nick shrugged.

"Who knows? It would seem the pair would stop at nothing to get their way."

Sam had a nagging thought in his head and spent a few moments trying to retrieve it. When he did, he couldn't understand it – it didn't make sense.

"Hang on a minute, this doesn't add up. Donna didn't know about my visit to Newquay. That was arranged at the last minute because I was going to be over here. So she couldn't have passed that information on. Unless that means it's bigger than just the two of them?"

That thought there might be more than one person who

was betraying them was terrifying and they all lapsed into thoughtful silence. The facts appeared to back it up though. Sam's mother had sprung the surprise trip to Tresco on him and it was decided that he would arrange to see the property in Newquay on the way back. He hadn't spoken to Donna since earlier that morning, well before he left London in his helicopter. In fact, he'd not had a conversation with her until the moment she'd arrived on the quayside. In that case, there was no way she could have known about the potential Newquay deal. Unless, unless…

A thought suddenly sprang into Sam's head which sent him racing across to a mahogany shelf where he'd left his phone charging. He snatched it from the socket and stabbed a dial button. Mel answered within seconds.

"Mel, this is important. You know the day that Donna came into the office and tricked you into believing there was a medical emergency downstairs. Which day was that?"

"I can tell you that exactly, which day it was. It was the afternoon of the day that you left for the Isles of Scilly with your mother."

"And what was it that you'd been doing before she arrived? I know it's a lot to ask, but can you remember?"

"Oh let me see now…."

Sam could almost hear Mel's mind whirring as she thought it through.

"I'd spoken to the Manchester conference organisers about the change of speaker…oh, and while I'd been doing that I'd had a missed call, so I listened to the message and noted that information down."

"And who was the message from?"

"It was the landlord in Newquay, the one with the derelict hotel that you were planning to look at on the way back. He'd called back to give me the address and the days and times when he was free to see you."

"And you noted all that down. On your notepad."

Sam was pacing up and down the deck, as his parents looked on.

"Well yes, of course, just as I always do," said Mel. "Sam what's this all about?"

"It's nothing to worry about, really Mel, nothing at all. Just one final question. Where would the notepad have been when Donna arrived?"

"Well next to my keyboard. I always lock everything away at night, or if I'm popping out but I had to race out for the medical emergency and there was no-one else in the office.....other than Donna."

The penny had dropped with Mel as to where this conversation was leading.

Sam thanked her and told her not to worry and to get back to her family. He ended the call and turned to his mother and Nick.

"When Donna was looking for the telephone number for the yacht, she would easily have seen the notes that Mel had on her desk. It would've been obvious what it was about and the name and contact details were there. It all makes sense. Donna is most definitely our leak."

*****

The conversation wasn't pretty, which surprised Sam. Given that Donna was already married to someone else, he'd thought that once the game was up she would throw in the towel and admit defeat.

At first there were the denials.

"I don't know what you mean. What are you talking about – married? How could I be married to anyone else? It's totally ridiculous."

"Donna I have it all here," Sam patted the manila envelope. "Dates, times, even photos. What more is there for me to know?"

"A photo!?"

Donna looked incredulous.

"Yes, a photo, albeit you were making an effort not to be seen. But you were there and all the other pieces have also fallen into place. I even have a copy of your marriage certificate. The game is up."

"What are you saying? You're ending it with me?"

Sam was astonished. Of course he was ending it with her, what did she think would happen?

From there things went downhill.

"Please don't," she pleaded. "I love you, we're great together."

"Don't be ridiculous. You're married to someone else."

"I made a mistake. I can get a divorce – a quickie divorce. I've not been with him since the honeymoon because I realised how strong *our* love was."

"If you love someone you don't cheat on them, let alone marry someone else while you're with them."

"It was a mistake…please!"

Donna was drumming her fists against his chest and he had to grab her arms to stop her.

"Enough Donna, enough. Don't embarrass yourself. It's over. And frankly it's unbelievable that you could ever imagine there's a way back from this. I could never marry you."

Donna took a step back. The crocodile tears dried up and were replaced by a nasty scowl.

"How dare you dump me," she said through gritted teeth. "How dare you. I'm going to make you pay for this Sam Kerchavel. I swear it."

"Make *me* pay. Make *me* pay! We haven't even started on you passing secrets from my business to your husband."

Donna had the good grace to pale at these words.

"I have confirmation on paper and a trail of times and dates but the look on your face tells me all I need to know."

Sam moved away from her and stood further along the deck. He couldn't bear to be near her.

"I…I don't know what you mean."

Sam rubbed his hair in exasperation.

"Donna at least have the good grace to admit it when you've been caught. You're lucky I haven't called the police. I'm still considering it. What you've done is illegal, Donna. Plain and simple."

Donna's eyes narrowed. She was like a wounded animal that had been cornered and she had every intention of fighting back.

"I suppose you're going to run off after Miss Goody Two-Shoes instead," she spat.

"I don't know who you mean."

"Yes you do. That Tara woman. The one with the ugly, dark gallery made of old bits of dried up drift wood."

Sam froze.

"How do you know what her gallery looks like?"

"I went to take a little look, didn't I. Once I saw that giant picture up in the lounge I knew something was up. Didn't take me long to find out what either. Did a bit of asking around. Ex-fiancée eh? You kept that quiet."

Sam felt a flicker of anger, matched with fear. He realised he should have been more honest but he had been working through his feelings for Tara. And it wasn't as if he'd come to the island to find her – he'd just stumbled across her. Now Donna was just trying to cover up for her own crimes and misdemeanours by muddying the waters. He wondered what on earth had happened when she'd visited the gallery.

"Anyway, she told me she had no intention of getting back with you, Sam Kerchavel. Said she was well shot of you the first time. Thought *I* was the one making a big mistake. Sounds like she was right."

So something had gone on then, some sort of confrontation? Sam doubted Donna's words, they weren't the kind of thing Tara would say to anyone, let alone a stranger - but even so the words hurt.

As soon as he realised that Donna had betrayed him, he had felt a huge sense of relief, followed by sheer elation. He'd held back from showing Tara his true feelings but the few days he had spent on the island had made him realise that he wanted her by his side. He was free to win her back, even if it meant competing for her affections against Chris. He still wasn't sure what role the other man played in Tara's life. Now he had a sinking feeling that Donna may have made his task more difficult.

"What business did you have going there?" he said through gritted teeth. "She has nothing to do with this."

"Oh, I think she has everything to do with it."

Donna reached into her large white bag and retrieved a tissue which she used to dab her eyes dramatically.

"I made a couple of mistakes Sam, that's all. We can still make it work, really we can. We're good together, we're meant to be."

"Do you think I could ever forget what you've done? Just put it behind me?" he raged. "Marry a woman who had not only lied and cheated with someone else, going as far as to marry him behind my back, but then worked with him to cheat my business? I have thousands of colleagues in my company, Donna and they all work very hard; you could have put their jobs at risk!"

"But just think what we could do if we work together, the millions we could make. Why, we could even turn this to our advantage – I could pretend to be an interested investor, you pull out, then I pull out and they'd have to accept a lower offer from you. Think of that Sam."

Donna's dark eyes gleamed with greed.

"No," Sam almost shouted. "No, that's not who I am Donna – you really don't know me at all, do you? Yes, I'm fortunate to have made a lot of money from my work, to be able to afford all of this," he gestured around the deck of The Aramat.

"But I would rather be penniless than rip people off, cheat them out of what is rightfully theirs. And that's why we could never work Donna, I couldn't bear to be married to someone like you who only has ice in their heart. Now if you don't get off my yacht in the next ten minutes, I will be calling the police and they'll take you off in handcuffs!"

His words struck Donna, just as surely as if she had been stung. Before she had a chance to say anything else, Sam walked over to the yacht's internal phone and spoke into it for a moment.

A minute later Philip arrived on the deck.

"Can you please accompany Donna down below and watch her pack, make sure she doesn't take anything, or make any calls," said Sam, ignoring Donna's indignant gasp.

He saw her eyes narrow with hatred. Then she picked up her bag, turned haughtily on her heels and marched off, with her nose in the air.

Shaken, Sam walked across to the bar and poured himself a large whisky. He didn't know why he had ever thought she would go quietly, it wasn't in her nature. It wasn't Sam she was going to miss, it was his money, but hopefully she had finally realised that the game was up.

Sure enough, after a few minutes she returned with her things. Philip headed to the bottom of the walkway and the launch.

"I'll call Mel, get her to send the helicopter to take you where you want to go," Sam said flatly. It wasn't generosity on his part, more a desire to get rid of her as soon as possible.

"And take Malcolm with you."

Sam had no intention of entertaining his former friend now that Donna was out of his life.

"I think he's busy at the moment," Donna said bitchily. "Of course, you know that something went on between him and your fiancée back in the day?"

Sam's jaw dropped open.

"What do you mean, something 'went on'?"

"I mean they had some sort of fling one afternoon when you were at work. I guess she was hedging her bets, seeing who was going to be the more successful one."

No, no, no, no, no, this couldn't be true, surely? Malcolm and Tara? Sam shook himself. He didn't believe it. Tara wasn't the type to cheat on him and even if she had, she would never have done so with Malcolm. His slimeball character was evident even then and she had always seemed uncomfortable when he was around.

'And yet, you saw them together didn't you? Having a fiery discussion in the café near your place the day before she did a runner,' doubt entered Sam's head.

He felt sick to his stomach, barely taking in what Donna was saying.

"Anyway, Malcolm thought he may as well take up where he left off. Get reacquainted," added Donna with a nasty sneer. "So I guess I might have to wait for him for a while. I've heard he likes to take things slow."

Sam felt a frisson of fear for Tara.

"Donna," he said in an ice cold voice. "This is important. Tell me what his plan is. Tell me where Malcolm is. Now!"

CHAPTER 16

Tara had a thumping headache by the end of the day, thanks to Donna's unpleasantness. What she needed was a long soak in a bath with a glass of wine and an early night. Chris had offered to oversee the gallery in the morning. He had plans for the following few days and so this was his only opportunity to help out. Not for the first time, Tara thought how blessed she was to have Chris in her life.

"I think a lie-in tomorrow is in order," Tara mused to Delilah. "A cup of tea in bed with some magazines. That way by the time we get up, Sam and that horrible Donna will be long gone."

Delilah whined a little; Tara wasn't sure if it was in sympathy or because she realised her morning walk was going to be a little later than usual.

She stared through the narrow windows for a moment at the cove beyond. Why was it that the sun seemed to shine a little brighter, the sand seemed even whiter than usual and the azure sea was an even deeper shade, now that Sam was on the island?

"It's just too bad," she said with a heavy sigh.

How she wished she'd never agreed to go to that

exhibition a few days before.

"I could easily have said no, have been the mystery artist behind the paintings."

Not that it would have made any difference. Sam would have realised they were created by her, just as surely as if she had placed her fingerprint in oils onto one of them. He had taken a keen interest in her work when they were together but it ran far deeper – as if their very souls were entwined and her work was as much a part of him, as it was of her.

Tara forced herself away from the view and busied herself with closing the gallery for the day. She washed up her mug and put it back on the shelf, then did a final check to make sure everything was in order, before calling to Delilah, putting her key in the lock and closing the door behind her.

She had her back to the pathway, as she fiddled with the lock. She really must get it sorted out because it was always tricky and Annabel had mentioned it to her several times.

Suddenly, someone had hold of her hair and she was yanked backwards, almost off her feet.

Delilah barked and Tara gave a little cry of pain, before a hand was clamped firmly over her mouth.

Then a voice - the voice of her nightmares - hissed close into her ear.

"Hello Tamara. Long time, no see."

Tara would have struggled, would have called out but for the fact she also felt the cold metal of a knife pressed against her throat.

*****

Sam could hear Delilah's frantic barking as he approached the gallery on his bike. Chris was already there and was starting to unlock the door hurriedly. The dog was obviously inside.

"Where's Tara?" Sam said frantically.

"I don't know," said Chris, with more than a hint of annoyance in his voice.

"I could hear Delilah barking so I've come over to see why. What's going on?"

"I think she might be in danger."

Chris pushed the door open and was immediately greeted by the anxious German Shepherd.

"OK girl, it's OK," he soothed.

Then: "Tara! Tara? Are you in here?"

The two men searched all the rooms in the gallery in record time but there was no sign of her. Sam headed back towards the front door but was stopped by Chris who grabbed hold of his jacket firmly.

"What's going on? Why do you think she's in danger?"

"I haven't got time to explain," said Sam angrily, pulling himself away.

Chris held fast.

"Make time," he growled. "Because she means everything to me too and whatever it is that's happened wouldn't have occurred if you weren't on the scene."

Sam was surprised at his words. Were his own feelings for Tara that obvious? And what exactly were Chris's towards her?

The last thing he needed right now was to do battle with the other man. Sam was a little taller and they were both broad and powerful but Tara had to be the priority. Besides, Chris knew the island better than he did and if they joined forces they could cover more ground.

"Can you help me?" he asked and Chris immediately nodded.

Sam quickly explained, realising as he did so how it seemed to leave more questions than answers but if he had them, Chris didn't waste time asking.

"I'll head over the ridge towards the Old Blockhouse and if needs be on towards Pentle Bay," he said. "You go head towards New Grimsby over the hillside. You know that way?"

Sam nodded.

"Good. Delilah's not been barking for long so I don't think they can have got too far. Is there any chance this Malcolm could be on a boat?"

"Unlikely I think," said Sam.

"OK well I will put in some calls to some of the locals and the coastguard and make sure that side is covered too."

Sam fished in his wallet for a business card, which he handed across.

"My phone number. Keep in touch. Call me if you find her."

It was Chris's turn to nod and he set off with Delilah who was on her lead but champing at the bit. Sam sincerely hoped the large dog could follow her mistress's scent. Heart pounding, he set off at a sprint up the footpath which led through the russet-coloured bracken.

*****

"What do you want with me, Malcolm?" asked Tara, as they made their way towards the top of the island. He was still holding the knife and was clutching her arm tightly, his breath coming out in short gasps. The years had not been kind to him, his skin was pale and he had put on a few pounds, his stomach hanging over his shorts and his body untoned. Whether it was adrenaline from his seizing Tara or the steepness of the hill, he sounded like he was struggling.

'Keep on your toes,' Tara said to herself. 'An opportunity to escape will come and you need to be ready to seize it.'

They had passed a couple earlier and it had crossed Tara's mind to call out but Malcolm had pressed the blade against her side and said: "Don't even think about it, for their sakes as well as yours."

The couple were obviously retired and Tara had no intention of putting them in danger. She tried to calm her mind, focus on her breathing and wait. The chance would surely come.

Eventually, they reached the top of the island and stopped. Malcolm slipped his arm around her neck again pressing the metal into her skin. He was looking around furtively, as if he was afraid that something – or someone was coming after him.

"Why don't you just let me go and we can forget all about this," Tara said weakly.

"I'll go back to the gallery, you can leave with Sam and his fiancée Donna and no-one will be any the wiser. I won't say a word about it."

Tara could only assume that Sam had invited his old

room-mate onto the island, even though he had implied they weren't in touch – yet another untruth uttered from the mouth of Sam Kerchavel. Not that he was top of her list of concerns at the moment.

Even so, Malcolm's next outburst surprised her.

"There is no Sam and Donna, thanks to you," he stormed.

Despite her predicament and her misgivings about Sam, Tara's heart lifted at the words. Was it really true? Might Sam still hold a torch for her?

"What do you mean and what's it got to do with me?" she asked, feeling Malcolm's stale breath, heavy and laboured on the back of her neck.

His body was pressed against hers and it made her feel nauseous. She forced herself to focus on the sound of the sea and the crying of the gulls above, anything to step out of her current predicament.

"I mean just that," Malcolm snarled. "Thanks to you Sam has split up with Donna. You've messed up all my plans *again.*"

"I don't know what you're talking about. What plans? Look, why don't you put the knife down and we can discuss it like rational human beings. I'm sure there's a perfectly good explanation."

"Oh there's a perfectly good explanation alright – you! Sam never could quite get over you and now he's ditched Donna to prove it."

"But why should you care about whether he ditched Donna?"

"Because she's my cousin, you idiot," Malcolm was so enraged that Tara hardly dared to breathe.

Her head was whirling. Donna was related to Malcolm? That would explain how Donna had found out that she used to be engaged to Sam.

"She's my cousin and was my ticket back into Sam's world, the world that I deserve. The world that you stuffed up for me the first time around. He and I were friends right through school and then college and were planning to go into business together," Malcolm waved the knife around dramatically whilst still holding onto Tara tightly.

"Just picture it, the two of us side by side. We would have made even more money together than Sam has on his own."

Tara doubted that. The fact was that Malcolm was too lazy even when they were younger to put in the work that Sam did, instead he was busy chasing girls and drinking heavily. From the look of him he hadn't put in much of an effort since either. Any success would have been Sam's alone, but Malcolm felt entitled to a cut.

"Of course all our plans were ruined when you came along and turned his head six years ago. Everything went out of the window."

"*You* came to the student art exhibition and brought him with you," Tara retorted, despite the predicament she was in. "Sam didn't even want to go!"

"Yeah, so what? I thought there'd be plenty of girls there, maybe there'd be a one night stand in it for me. I was trying to encourage Sam to do the same, he was always so straight-laced. But of course then he stumbles across you."

Tara allowed herself a faint smile. Despite Malcolm's grubby efforts, Sam hadn't followed down the same path. It cheered her a little.

"Given you knew Sam's character it's a wonder you risked it. There was always the chance that he would find someone to have a relationship with which could then come between you."

Malcolm snorted and Tara realised she had hit a nerve. He obviously felt that no matter who came into Sam's life, he would be the most important. The arrogance of the man! No wonder he had always been so cold towards her.

"Well why didn't you two pick up where you left off when I was out of the picture? Back to being best buddies?"

Malcolm made some sort of guttural growl and pressed the knife blade deeper against her. If she so much as moved a millimetre it would cut her.

"You'd cast some kind of spell over him, that's why," he hissed again. "Things didn't go back to normal afterwards. Despite all my efforts, Sam didn't want to know. Thanks to you."

'Thanks to sensing there was something dodgy about you, more like!' thought Tara.

"But then I had a second chance with Donna; after all she's as ambitious as I am. She wanted to get into property development because of the large dividends and I knew as soon as I introduced her to Sam that she would see his potential. Always been one for the main chance, my cousin."

She felt him move behind her as he wiped the sweat from his face with his sleeve.

'Next time,' thought Tara. 'Next time he moves like that I'll be ready for him. I'll need to keep him talking and then I can make my move.'

At least for now Malcolm was still telling her his story and as long as he did, she would probably be OK. It was when he stopped and was faced with a choice as to what to do that worried her. She had to seize her chance before then!

"If Donna hadn't gone and got her boyfriend involved we'd probably have made it too. She just had to marry Sam and then she and I would have had access to all that wealth. Think what we could have done with it. Just think!"

Malcolm's greed made Tara feel sick. Fancy pretending to be Sam's friend for all those years and setting him up with a younger cousin, just so they could get their hands on everything that he had worked so hard for. It was disgusting. And Donna already had a boyfriend? Had Sam discovered it which led to the split? If not, she would have to tell him – if she ever got out of this mess. Tears pricked her eyes. What if she never saw Sam again? Leaving all those years ago had been the right thing to do, after she'd discovered he hadn't been honest with her. But the pain had been excruciating, knowing that she wouldn't set eyes on that handsome face. If she didn't tread carefully now, she might never see him again, or anyone else for that matter.

Suddenly a thought dawned on her.

"So that day in the café....that was all a ruse to try to get rid of me?"

"Finally she gets it! Yes, it was a way to get you out of our lives. And maybe to have a little fun into the bargain too,"

Malcolm said breathing heavily into her ear and he started to run his other hand down Tara's throat and towards the opening in her shirt. She froze, trying to hold down the nausea she was feeling.

"A man has needs, especially when he comes across a beautiful woman like you. And why should Sam have all the fun?"

"Let her go!"

CHAPTER 17

"Let her go!"

Sam's shout was so loud that they both jumped. Unfortunately, it wasn't enough for Malcolm to loosen his grip on the knife. Instead, holding tightly on to her, Malcolm spun them both around. Standing a few feet from them, his face pale and drawn, was Sam. Despite this and everything that was going on Tara felt that her heart would explode in her chest. He was breathing heavily as if he had run up the steep hill from Old Grimsby, searching for her. His handsome face was taut with fear and his deep blue eyes searched her face, questioning her. She gave the faintest nod in reply and a small smile, to confirm that she was unharmed. A flicker of relief crossed his face.

"Come on Malcolm, it's me you want," Sam said firmly. "Me you've got a beef with. This has nothing to do with Tara, so just let her go."

"Tara? Who the hell is Tara?" Malcolm said and then peered round to look her in the face.

"Oh, changed your name did you? No wonder lover boy couldn't find you. You must've been that keen to get away from him."

Tara said nothing. She wasn't going to satisfy the man with a reply, or risk antagonising him any further. As welcome as Sam's arrival was, it did mean one thing – her offer to Malcolm of his leaving quietly and this incident never being mentioned again had gone out of the window. The stakes were now much higher, police involvement an inevitability, however it played out. Malcolm may be lazy but he wasn't a stupid man and would realise that. It made her predicament all the more precarious.

"Malcolm, come on. Be sensible, let her go."

Sam was inching towards them carefully, his hand outstretched imploringly.

"Don't be ridiculous," said Malcolm calmly. "There's no walking away from this one. And so I would stay right where you are, Sam Kerchavel, unless you want to risk the knife slipping and damaging this pretty face."

With that, he moved the blade from Tara's throat and pressed it against her cheek.

Sam froze in horror.

"OK, OK I'm staying right here! Don't hurt her. OK I won't come any nearer. I promise."

"Aww did-dums are you worried about her?" Malcolm sneered. "Give me one good reason why I shouldn't do it, eh? After all it's all her fault. She's managed to thwart my plans not once, but twice."

Tara watched Sam's jaw tighten.

"Right through school we had plans, were destined to be business partners. We had it all mapped out, were going to make billions together, rule the world. Then she comes along and turns your head and next thing I'm out in the cold. Took all my ingenuity to get rid of her the first time. Now I discover that Tamara or Tara or whoever the hell she is, is back. And surprise, surprise Donna is now out in the cold."

"What do you mean, it took all your ingenuity to get rid of her the first time?" Sam asked coldly. "What did you have to do with it?"

Sam always suspected that his friend knew more about Tara's disappearance than he was letting on. After all, he saw them the afternoon before she left and they seemed to be having words, though Malcolm had insisted it was over a friend of hers. Sam could never prove otherwise but the relationship, which had already been cooling, fell off a cliff. And here they were standing near one, with the final act playing out.

Malcolm certainly seemed to be enjoying the drama of it all and his position in centre stage.

"It was so easy. I pity you two really. Suckers! I mean, you were supposed to have the perfect relationship, were planning to get married for goodness' sake and yet I was able to break you in two just like that."

He clicked his thumb and a finger together.

Sam's eyes had been fixed on Malcolm for the whole of the conversation, Tara hoped because he was seeking an opportunity to get her out of his grip. But now he looked at her and their eyes locked. What could she see in those warm blue pools? Regret? An apology? She gave him a brief, encouraging smile.

"Luckily for me I knew everything about you Sam

Kerchavel and all your little secrets. All I had to do was find out a bit more about her."

He pushed Tara forward a step, whilst still maintaining his grip and keeping the blade pressed against her face, as if to emphasis who he was talking about. Tara felt the knife make the lightest sharp nick into her skin. She tried not to panic but concentrated instead on taking a couple of long deep breaths. Hopefully it was only a scratch because to react now could be fatal.

'He's getting too cocky, he's going to make a mistake. And when he does, you have to be ready Tara Hemsworth. Until then stay calm. The main thing is that you both come out of it alive.'

"…..quick to tell me all about her and tell me all her vulnerabilities."

Tara realised she had missed a part of Malcolm's story but it would seem he had revealed the person who had told him all about her. She suspected it was Sue, her own roommate, who had been quite taken with Malcolm for a while; they'd been out on a couple of dates. Knowing how manipulative he was, Sue could quite easily have spilled personal stuff about Tara without realising the harm she was doing.

"It was so easy," said Malcolm and Tara could feel his chest swell a little as he started to boast.

"I soon discovered that the one big issue was trust because she was all alone in the world. Poor Mummy and Daddy were dead."

Tara swallowed hard. Any mention of her beloved

parents still hurt like heck but to hear them uttered by this vile man knocked her for six. Which is exactly what Sam looked like he wanted to do to Malcolm. He was no longer watching her and she hoped that he hadn't noticed the blood that she could feel trickling down her face. She didn't want him to make any sudden moves out of anger and risk his own life. For the moment Sam was very still, staring at Malcolm intensely, a look of sheer loathing on his face.

"No brothers or sisters either, poor lamb. So when she met the dashing and soon to be incredibly wealthy Sam Kerchavel, she must've thought all her Christmases had come at once."

"It wasn't like that!" Tara blurted out angrily and she saw Sam start. He gestured with his hand for her to keep calm but it was too late. Malcolm jerked her body backwards hard against him, pulling her face next to his.

"Oh wasn't it? You're telling me that you didn't clap eyes on him and think what he could do for you? He was already making some money and it was pretty obvious he and I would do well in the future. All the women seemed to think he was handsome too. Perfect for little Miss Orphan, wasn't he."

"No!" said Tara, defiantly. "No. There was no way I was going to go for a man because of his prospects. That would be unfair to him and the height of insecurity – risk making each other unhappy and then end up with a divorce? No way. I was with Sam because I loved him."

She wanted to add that she still did love him but felt it was too soon. Up until a few hours ago Sam was engaged to someone else.

"Ahhh how sweet," said Malcolm sarcastically. "Didn't take much for you to mistrust him and run away though, did it?"

Tara sagged against him. It was hard to re-live the 24 hours before her disappearance. She and Sam were so happy and she had genuinely believed nothing could ever come between them. When she'd met with Malcolm at his request the afternoon before she left, she thought he wanted to congratulate her on their engagement. She was wrong.

"That recording though…the one you played me….It was Sam speaking. And the pictures."

"Yes but you were right not to believe it. Took me ages to get that sorted. Weeks and weeks of recording snippets of conversation and putting them together. You wouldn't believe the number of times I had to ditch material because a background noise suddenly disappeared, or the words didn't quite fit together. The pictures were a bit easier. You should both be flattered that I went to so much effort."

"What recording?" Sam demanded. "What pictures?"

"I saw Malcolm the day before I left," Tara's voice was thick with misery. "That time you saw us in the café. He said he was a friend and needed to warn me off marrying you. That you were only after me as a bit of arm candy. Then he played me a recording of you, which seemed to back it up."

"A recording of *me*?" Sam was incredulous. "Saying what? There was no way you were ever arm candy or anything remotely like it, Tara. I would never have thought of any woman like that, least of all you. Never."

His face was so earnest that she suddenly realised to her

horror that she had been mistaken all those years ago. Her heart dropped like a stone. What had she done?! She had walked out on the only man she had ever loved, the person who had won her heart completely. By believing Malcom's lies she had destroyed it all. Tara felt sick to the stomach.

"All I had to do was record a few of our conversations over the course of several weeks and edit them together," Malcolm explained matter of factly. "It did mean drawing you into a few conversations. The one where you said you'd not been looking for anything serious was particularly useful."

"But I went on to say that she'd bowled me over, that I never expected to meet my future wife when we went out that night!" Sam protested. "I remember that conversation. I couldn't work out why you were asking me all of these strange questions when we were just meant to be relaxing in front of the TV with a beer. You were setting me up! Setting us both up!"

Malcolm just laughed, a sinister, creepy laugh. Tara had a sense that he thought he had the upper hand, so pleased was he with the way he had gone about destroying the young couple. While it made her feel angry and devastated in equal measure, her head was telling her that this could be her best chance of escape from his clutches.

"To be fair though, she didn't quite believe it," her captor added. "Even when I showed her photos of you kissing and hugging other women."

"Kissing and hugging other women!? I wouldn't...I couldn't!....," Sam protested.

"Your cousin's party? The school reunion? I was taking some photos remember? As well as taking the nice group shots that you saw, I also made sure I took one or too which seemed to imply something else. I was planning on adding a date stamp to the photos but fortunately you wore the new shirt to one that you had chosen with Tara, so she knew they were taken since she'd been on the scene."

Tara heard Sam take in a deep breath but Malcolm continued oblivious.

"I was banking – rightly – on the fact that you wanted to introduce her to your parents before your cousins, so Tara didn't go and therefore wouldn't understand why you were embracing one or two lovely other women. A slight turn of the camera angle can make things appear very damaging indeed."

Sam was speechless. His hatred of Malcolm could not be greater than it was at this point but he was also astonished at the amount of planning his former friend had put into making sure he got Tara off the scene. If he had ever put that much effort into actually holding down a job, he could've got somewhere in life.

"And still she didn't believe me! Can you imagine that Sam? I had to employ my trump card to convince her. Well two actually."

"Which were?" Sam asked coldly.

"I said that if she didn't believe me she should ask you one particular question. I showed her the answer and said if you lied to her face that would prove I was right. I told her what the question was and she asked it. And surprise,

surprise you didn't tell her the truth. Of course I also suggested that we two could get together once you were out of the picture."

Malcolm stroked Tara's arm with these words and she shuddered. Sam took an angry step forward, causing Malcolm to move the knife to her throat.

"Ah, ah, not so hasty. If it's any consolation she didn't seem so keen on that idea, even though I made her a substantial offer in return for one or two, *favours...*"

Tara shuddered at the memory. She could recall in full detail what the favours were that Malcolm had suggested. He'd reminded her how alone she was in the world, how rocky a career in the arts could be and how she could offset that instability by hooking up with him when he fancied it. After all, he was going to be a business partner of Sam's with access to all the wealth Sam was bound to accrue. The memory made her feel physically sick. She could remember being incredulous, still not wishing to believe the recording, or the photos that Sam appeared in. Surely her Sam, the love of her life was true? Surely their love wasn't built on a lie? He couldn't be faking these feelings, could he?

"And so your last meeting, that evening at dinner. It was soooo sweet! Sam told me beforehand that he was going to tell you everything that had happened to him and his mother. But just as he started you got in first didn't you."

Malcolm jerked Tara again roughly, causing Sam to step forward again, then stop.

Tara remembered how Sam had taken her hand in the cosy cubicle that he had chosen for their dinner and she had searched those beautiful blue eyes earnestly, trying to work out if he was genuine or not. He had started to say how he wanted to tell her something, something important about his life but Tara was too anxious to listen. Malcolm's words had been eating into her soul and she just wanted to know the answer to the question he had suggested she ask. The question that would show her, once and for all, if Sam was genuine or not.

"Sam," she had said coolly, placing her hand on his to interrupt him.

"Sam, you can tell me all this later. First I just have one question for you and it's an important one."

"Ask away," he had seemed puzzled by her interruption but had no clue as to the enormity of what was happening.

Tara had looked him straight in the eye.

"Have you ever been in trouble with the police?" she asked.

There was a beat, a moment's hesitation before he answered. And that had smashed her heart into a million pieces.

"No," he had replied.

And with that, her plans to leave were set.

CHAPTER 18

"But I was telling the truth," Sam protested. "I've never been in trouble with the police."

"Ah smoke and mirrors Sam, smoke and mirrors," Malcolm smiled. "Because you *were* arrested, weren't you. And luckily for me, as well as you telling me all about it, there was also a report of that arrest in the paper. I thought that it might come in handy in the future and so I cut it out and kept it."

"You did what!" Sam spluttered with rage. "You kept that report for all those years, even though you were my closest friend and knew exactly what had gone on? How dare you!"

Malcolm merely shrugged.

Tara was trying to keep up.

"What are you saying? That the newspaper report wasn't true?"

"Oh it was true," said Sam heavily.

"So you were in trouble with the police, then," Tara retorted, a hint of accusation in her voice.

She had been right after all. Sam had told her a bare-faced lie, right to her face and coupled with the recording and the photos she had been shown, that had been all she needed. Malcolm was right that she hadn't had many people to turn to, but her mother's oldest friend Annabel lived on the Isles of Scilly. Tara had been captivated by the beauty of the place as a small child and had realised it might provide the solace she needed, while she tried to get over Sam and escaped Malcolm. Five years later it was still home.

"I was arrested briefly but I was never actually in trouble with the police."

Sam's voice cut through her thoughts. He sounded weary.

"I was going to tell you the whole story over dinner that evening."

He shifted uneasily from foot to foot. Whatever he was going to say would be hard enough in usual times, without the deceitful Malcolm there to witness it.

Sam looked down at the ground for a few moments and then looked Tara straight in the eye. Pain was etched across to his face and she ached for him. She put a hand out towards him, to offer what little comfort she could.

"My father was abusive to my mother," he said at last.

"She kept it very well hidden when I was small, making sure she was the one who took the full brunt of his mind games and his fists."

He spat out the last few words with anger.

"It was tough because my father spent all our money on drink and gambling and sometimes we had to move from place to place. But I thought despite that they got along OK. She was very good at hiding the true horror of it from me and more than made up for it by smothering me with love and happy memories."

Tara thought of the graceful Elizabeth. There was no sign of what she must have endured, both physical and mental. To have gone through all that and keep it hidden from Sam was astonishing. Once again she felt the tears pricking the back of her eyes.

"However, as I got older, I started to hear whispers and I got into trouble at primary school for fighting with a boy who said those rumours out loud. Unfortunately, I didn't believe him so told my parents and later Mum got it even worse, for not covering it up well enough."

Sam kicked at a piece of fern with his boot. Even though it was not his fault he still blamed himself.

"Anyway, when I was 13, I won a scholarship to boarding school, which unfortunately was where I met him," he nodded towards Malcolm, unwilling to speak his name. Malcolm merely snorted.

"Mum was really keen for me to go and I was hurt at the time. It felt like she wanted to get rid of me. I didn't realise that it was her way of trying to protect me. So I went and academically I did well and got into rugby and other things and grew up. I tried not to go home too often. It was pretty obvious my dad was drinking heavily and I was still angry with Mum."

Sam's voice cracked on the last few words. He had always regretted the times they could have spent together, had he realised how much his mother loved him. Perhaps too he could have stopped things sooner? He looked so sad that

Tara had to blink back her tears.

"Oh spare us the sob story and just tell her," Malcolm said nastily. "She'll want to know it all before she goes."

It was the first time that Malcolm had hinted as to the outcome of this standoff and it jolted Tara back to reality. Sam looked panic stricken.

"Go on," urged Malcolm. "Tell her everything."

Sam carried on, though his face had paled.

"I came back one Saturday unexpectedly. My rugby game had been cancelled and a few of my friends had gone home. I'd been running this dog walking business and had an idea to expand but needed a bit of investment, so was planning to ask Mum if she had stashed any funds - money that dad hadn't drunk away."

Tara nodded encouragingly, as best she could in the circumstances.

"I wanted to surprise her, so I snuck in through the back door. It was then that I could hear a commotion from the kitchen, glasses and plates being smashed, so I ran around. I really thought I would come across a burglar.

"But there was my dad, wiping his hands having just beaten-up Mum. She was covered in blood."

Sam shuddered at the thought.

"I flew at him. I don't know if he saw me coming but I rugby tackled him. We ended up fighting on the floor. Mum called the police. He was giving as good as he got, raining blows down on me, just as he had on her. But I got some in too and because I was younger and stronger, mine hurt him more. Turns out I broke a couple of his ribs in the fall and then broke his nose. Those were the worst things."

He looked earnestly at Tara.

"When the police came, he told them I'd come home and assaulted both of them and he'd been trying to stop me. The police had no choice but to arrest me too."

Tara gave a little gasp.

"What did your mum say?"

"She told them the truth but the police had to arrest both of us and then try to sort it out. Luckily for me, as well as Mum's testimony, one of the neighbours had heard Dad shouting and the sound of things breaking, then saw me enter the garden gate a few minutes later. She'd also heard him beating up my Mum several times before but was too scared to say anything."

He sighed heavily.

"My father insisted on my being charged but the police didn't want to do that; they thought we'd been through enough. I was released without charge, though not before the local newspaper had run a piece which said two people had been arrested. Foolishly I trusted my best friend and showed him a copy of it when I got back to school. Little did I know he would keep it."

He looked accusingly at Malcolm who merely shrugged.

"Anyway, at least I was able to get Mum somewhere safe and then the two of us started again. We didn't see Dad again."

He looked steadily at Tara again.

"So I was telling the truth when I said that I hadn't been in trouble with the police, although it took them a few hours to release me from custody. Although I can understand what with the tape, photos and the newspaper cutting, Malcolm made it seem very convincing that I was lying."

Tara's heart ached. All this time she could have been with Sam, could've been his wife, were it not for Malcolm's scheming – playing on her and Sam's vulnerabilities.

"I will give you two one piece of credit though," Malcolm said suddenly. "She took a lot of persuasion, my hardest task ever. She did have real faith in you and it took everything I had to convince her otherwise. And as for Sam," he added, addressing Tara.

"...well he was never the same again. Even after the lovely Donna came along. So even I must admit that you two really loved each other."

"Love."

Sam spoke so softly that Tara thought she had misheard.

"What did you say?" snapped Malcolm.

"Love," said Sam in a clearer, loud voice. "We *still* love each other. At least I certainly do. My feelings haven't changed and I realised that when I first made you jump at the art exhibition and you cut your hand."

Tara rubbed her hand instinctively where it was healing over. It was only a few days ago but seemed like a million light years.

"I still love you Tara. How about you?"

Sam looked at her with such hope that her heart melted there and then. He loved her! After all that had gone on between them, after she had left him because of Malcolm's lies – *Sam Kerchavel still loved her*! Her biggest, broadest smile broke across her face.

"I love you too," she said happily.

Their words had a sudden impact on Malcolm.

"Shut up!" he snapped at Sam. "Shut up and stop this nonsense. You are never going to win I tell you, never!"

As he shouted the words he took the knife away from Tara's body for a moment and started to wave it towards Sam. It was the chance she had been waiting for.

Quick as a flash, she brought her elbow back as hard as possible into Malcolm's ribs, winding him and causing him to double over. Before he'd had a chance to recover, she brought her knee up to connect firmly with his face and then pushed him away from her, as hard as she could.

Sam had already sprung into action and as Malcolm started to fall he rugby tackled him, barrelling into the other man and grabbing his wrist which held the knife.

"Run Tara, run!" he shouted as he wrestled the blade away.

Sam was the stronger and fitter man but Malcolm's heavy body wasn't helping. Even so, Sam managed to prise the knife from his grasp and then tossed it away as far as he could. He then wrestled with Malcolm to pin him down and prevent his escape.

He turned for a moment and saw Tara standing near them, holding the knife.

"Tara please go - it's not safe."

"I'm not leaving you!" she shouted back.

"It's fine, I'll be fine. I'll hold on to him until you get the police."

Sam had pinned Malcolm's arms down but his former

friend was still struggling beneath him. It would be easier if he were to knock him out cold but Sam wasn't sure that he could control the white rage that had built up within him as he had watched the man threaten Tara's life. And he didn't want to turn out like his father. This would have to do for now. Hopefully some help could be summoned quickly.

"It's OK," said Tara suddenly. "You can let him go now Sam. We've got it covered."

Sam turned his head in surprise. Although he was glad of the help, his heart sank a little when he saw Chris running towards them. Then he realised that it wasn't Chris Tara was looking at. He followed her train of sight to Delilah who was also racing towards them, barking as she did so. As the dog reached them Tara said:

"Sam, step away, we've got this."

He looked at her with puzzlement, whilst still trying to quell the struggling Malcolm.

"Honestly Sam, please trust me. You have to move away. *Now.*"

Sam wasn't totally sure what was going on but if he truly loved Tara he also knew he had to trust her implicitly. He sprang away quickly, giving Malcolm an extra shove as he did so to leave him sprawling in the grass.

Immediately Tara called: "Delilah, hold!"

To his astonishment the dog raced towards Malcolm, teeth bared and growling. Malcolm scrambled back a few feet but the German Shepherd kept close, almost daring him to make a run for it. If he did, Sam was pretty sure Delilah would bring him down.

"What sort of a savage is that? Keep it away from me!" screamed Malcolm, who was white with fear.

"That 'savage' is actually a former police dog and she's trained to keep prisoners right where they are until her colleagues arrive!" declared Tara proudly.

Sam ran across to her and pulled her into his arms.

"Are you OK?" he said. He saw the blood on her cheek. "Tara, you're hurt. Let me look."

"It's nothing, just a little nick. Honestly."

"I thought I might lose you forever," groaned Sam, his face pinched with agony. "I honestly thought he might kill you and you'd be lost to me forever."

"Nope, still here," she laughed.

"Don't joke about it," Sam held her face in his hands whilst avoiding the injury she had sustained.

His stunning blue eyes bored into hers. "I never want to go through anything like that again."

"Nor do I," said Tara breathlessly.

"And I never want to lose you again either. Not for one minute. I meant what I said…I love you. Always have, always will. I have one thing to thank Malcolm for – I was so scared that I might lose you and so I had to say it, had to let you know what you mean to me. But if you don't feel the same, if you said you loved me back then to get us out of that fix, well I'd understand. Though I hope you at least realise that I never betrayed you."

"I'm so sorry," Tara said and she immediately saw Sam's face fall. He took a step back, a look of devastation on his face.

"I see," he said gravely.

"No, you don't understand," she laughed again, pulling him back towards her. "I was saying I'm sorry that I doubted you, sorry that I believed that snake Malcolm. Sorry that I left."

Sam's handsome features relaxed with relief.

"Oh thank goodness. And don't say sorry – we were both manipulated by him. He played a very clever game."

"I'd lost my parents just a couple of years before that and still felt very vulnerable. I did feel alone until you came along. The thought that it might not be real, might not be true, well I think he just played on my deepest fears…"

Tara's eyes swam with tears.

"Hey, shush, shush, it was real, I was true. Damn it, it is real and I am still true to you."

"But what about Donna?"

"Gone. Out of my life. I mean for a start it turns out she was married to someone else."

Tara gasped with shock. Sam chuckled at her reaction.

"Yes, it was a bit of a surprise but it was going to end anyway. After all you can't marry someone…when you're in love with another person."

With that Sam's lips found hers and all the fear and sadness and heartache of the past five years were washed away as clearly as the new tide on the sand, as Tara lost herself in his deep embrace.

How long had they both waited for this moment? Before it had felt like they were the perfect couple but now their love was stronger, their need to be together like two ancient souls entwined. As Sam's kiss deepened, she felt him searching for her, tentatively at first before it grew into such passion that it threatened to overwhelm them both. Tara felt the tears stream down her face, mingling with the blood. Sam felt the wetness under his fingers and drew back from her.

"What is it?" he asked, his face full of concern.

"Relief," she said tearfully.

"He can't hurt you anymore."

"No, I didn't mean that," Tara's voice was choked with sobs. "I mean relief that we have found our way back to one another. Is it true Sam? Is it real?"

"Yes, my darling girl," he said smiling at her before kissing away the tears on her cheeks. "Yes, it is. And believe me when I say I'm going to spend every second of every day making sure you never have any cause to doubt us again."

CHAPTER 19

The thwump, thwump, thwump of an approaching helicopter caused Tara and Sam to look up.

As it drew nearer, making the gorse and bracken bend and weave, they saw it belonged to the police. Chris had obviously alerted them as to what had happened on the island.

Malcolm saw it too and tried to scramble away but Delilah barked and growled, making sure he stayed right where he was.

Two police officers - a man and a woman - jumped out, as soon as the helicopter touched down, ducking beneath the rotor blades and racing towards them.

When the policeman was ready, Tara called Delilah away from guarding Malcolm and immediately a set of handcuffs was slapped onto him. He was unceremoniously pulled to his feet and escorted towards the waiting helicopter, his eyes fixed on the ground to avoid contact with either Tara or Sam. There were no parting words, there was nothing more to be said.

As Malcolm disappeared on board, Sam turned to find the

police woman was behind them, kissing Chris passionately!

"That's Laura, Chris's girlfriend," Tara explained.

"She's the local police officer here but she's been away on a training course for a couple of weeks. I guess they thought they'd bring her back at the same time as making their arrest!"

Sam was stunned.

"But I thought Chris had the hots for you?"

"For me? Don't be ridiculous!" it was Tara's turn to look astonished.

"Yes, for you. He was always there, always so protective of you."

"That's because they're two of my closest friends. Chris was in the police force and then left to set up his own self-defence business on the island, among other things. Where do you think I got my moves from?"

And with that Tara did a light karate-style kick towards him.

"Well, that was impressive, how you took Malcolm on. Dangerous though," Sam was half in awe, half scolding her.

"I couldn't leave it all to you now, could I!"

They were interrupted by the helicopter's engines starting up again. The sound was deafening and the force of the rotor blades temporarily flattened the grass and the bracken around them again. Tara shielded her eyes and also put a reassuring hand on Delilah's head, although the dog didn't seem remotely bothered. The three of them stood side by side and watched as it lifted up and headed across the water towards the mainland.

Soon silence returned and a troubled frown crossed Sam's face.

"So, the self-defence…Delilah…?"

Tara's smile faded a little.

"When I came here I was scared," she admitted. "Malcolm had managed to make me fear everything – even you…" she put her hand up to touch his cheek to reassure him that was no longer the case and he kissed her fingertips, savouring their softness.

"He said he would leave me alone if I left you but I wasn't convinced. Annabel was an old friend of my mother's and I knew she would take me in. Besides, I'd had such happy memories spent here as a child. I dropped the name Tamara – that was just some silly nonsense that my friends at college had persuaded me to use because they thought it sounded more exotic for an artist than Tara…"

Sam spluttered in indignation.

"I know, right? What's wrong with Tara? I used my real first name and took on my mother's maiden name as a surname and voila! I had a whole new life.

"The problem was I still couldn't sleep at night, still feared what might happen if Malcolm ever turned up. After a while I was tired of being scared. I'd already met Chris and Laura and so asked them to teach me some moves."

"They were very impressive," Sam said pulling her towards him and nuzzling into her neck.

He still couldn't believe that he was able to do this, to touch her and hold her close after all this time…

Suddenly he heard a loud bark and turned to see Delilah

standing in front of them. She was wagging her tail but she was obviously unsure as to why this man was suddenly holding on to her mistress so tightly.

"Don't worry," Tara broke away to bend down and reassure her dog. "He's harmless...mostly."

"Mostly harmless, well that's something for my resume," Sam said, laughing.

"And was Delilah part of the plan?"

"Not really. Chris told me one day about a young police dog that had been injured just a couple of weeks away from the end of her training. They didn't think she would recover her strength enough to perform the role."

"She seemed pretty strong when she was racing over to guard Malcolm."

"Yes, she's done well," Tara stroked the soft coat and was rewarded with a wagging tail.

"Though she still does limp occasionally and so they were right to pension her off."

"But what a coincidence – the name."

Sam had been hung up on the dog's name since he had arrived. Hardly anyone knew that his full name was Samson.

"Yes, well would you believe her first name was... Tamara! Not only did it remind me of my past but it was too close to Tara and so I needed a new name for her. I couldn't think of anyone who had taken on a 'Malcolm' before but there was a case of someone taking on a Samson."

"Not necessarily the greatest example!"

"No, true," she said. "But it reminded me that she was here as my protector and at the time, it was what I needed.

I'm not sure who rescued who to be honest."

Sam suddenly looked downcast.

"I'm so sorry that you felt that way about me…that you thought for one second I could betray you. And even sorrier that that slimeball," he jerked his thumb in the direction that the helicopter had taken,

"…could've frightened you so much. It must've been awful."

"It was," admitted Tara, chewing her lip thoughtfully. "Had it happened at a different time then it wouldn't have worked. But it was so close to losing my parents. I should've given you a chance but I felt really alone."

"You don't have to feel alone again," Sam said, taking her in his arms. "I'm going to be right here by your side. Though I do have a question for you."

"Ask me anything."

"Have you told anyone else on the island that my full name is Samson? I mean I'd hate for them to make the connection with the dog, that would raise a few eyebrows."

"Well wouldn't you like to know!" Tara laughed tapping the side of her nose.

"Yes, I would," Sam said mischievously. "And I'm going to find ways to make you tell me."

With that he bent his head down to bestow upon her a long, sweet, loving kiss. Tara never wanted it to end.

"Ahem!"

They were interrupted by Chris and his police officer girlfriend, Laura, who were now standing a few feet away.

Sam immediately broke away from Tara and put his hand out to shake Chris's.

"I'm sorry Chris," he said earnestly. "I misjudged you. I thought...well it doesn't really matter what I thought. I'm just grateful to both of you," he nodded towards Laura.

"Grateful that you helped Tara. That you were good friends to her and taught her the skills that probably saved her life just now."

Sam's voice was full of emotion as he said this and Tara thought it best to lighten the mood.

"Yes, I think you'll find I did all the hard work in tackling Malcolm and you just came in at the end and took the glory," she laughed.

"I don't know about that," Sam retorted. "To be honest I think it was Delilah who took centre stage."

They all laughed until Chris said seriously,

"I hope you're not going to hurt Tara again. Things were pretty rough for her for a while."

"No," said Sam levelly, looking the other man in the eye. "I won't. I hadn't realised what Malcolm had done...I did try to find you," he turned back towards Tara.

"I searched for years for you, high and low. In the end I just thought you didn't want to be found because you didn't want *me* anymore. That was the question I wanted to ask you that night in the gallery. I wanted to know why you had done it, why you had left with no word, no warning, when we were both so happy. Now I can see it all, the whole picture."

"And so can I," she said softly, her large brown eyes glistening.

Dusk was beginning to fall and a peace had settled over the land again.

"We should head back before it gets dark. Besides, I need someone to look at the cut on your cheek and no doubt there are police statements to complete," said Sam. "One thing's for sure, I intend to make sure Malcolm doesn't get away with what he did today."

He held out his hand to Tara.

"Coming?"

"You bet!" she said happily, as she slipped her hand into his.

CHAPTER 20

"Where have you been?" Tara asked nervously.

She'd headed across to Sam's luxury holiday apartment just as soon as she was up the next day, only to be told that he had gone out. So she'd gone back to her gallery and opened for business, spending a few anxious hours waiting for him to return.

The previous night they had made their way back to the harbour where The Aramat was moored, to be greeted by an anxious Elizabeth and Nick. Once they had reassured them, Sam took Tara to see the nurse before they gave their police statements to Laura. It led to a late dinner, where they recounted the whole story to the older couple. Tara was so delighted to have met Elizabeth and Nick properly. The trio was very close but they welcomed her with open arms.

"But maybe I dreamt it all, given that he seems to have done a disappearing act already," she said to Delilah. The dog gave her an understanding whine.

Suddenly Sam burst in through the door, sprinted across the room to Tara and lifted her up into his arms before devouring her with a long, deep kiss. It was a long time before she could draw breath to find out where he had gone.

"I've been to St Martin's," he told her.

"What on earth for?"

There were plenty of reasons to explore the beautiful neighbouring island of St Martin's, which Tara loved to see from the spectacular gallery windows, but it seemed a strange destination for Sam to make on his own. All very cloak and dagger.

"Come with me and I will explain," Sam said, putting his hand out to her, a broad grin across his face.

"Can't you tell me here? Annabel has lots of guests in and Chris is spending time with Laura, so there's no-one else to run the gallery."

"Put the 'closed' sign across."

"I'm sorry?"

"Let's go crazy for once and put the 'closed' sign across. Shut the gallery and take some time off. We had quite an adventure yesterday and both work too hard, so it's time we had a little fun. Besides this is a special occasion."

Tara stared at him in surprise. Was this really the multi-millionaire Sam Kerchavel talking? The businessman who worked every hour to become a success, suggesting time off?

"Well…I suppose I could, take an hour or so," she said slowly.

"That's my girl," he said.

Then a more serious look crossed his handsome features.

"To be honest, after you left and I couldn't find you, I threw myself into my work. It made me very successful but it never made me feel whole, however much I tried to kid myself. Now that we're together, I think it's time to step back a little."

He pulled her into his arms and kissed the tip of her nose. Once again she felt lost as she drowned in those beautiful blue eyes.

"So please…close the gallery for me. I really want to tell you about my trip."

He dropped some more kisses on her cheeks and forehead. It was all he could do to stop himself working his way down her neck, his tongue running along her smooth skin….

"OK OK!" she laughed, struggling out of his arms.

With that the door opened and a couple came into the shop. Tara pushed Sam away and he had to wait a frustrating 30 minutes while they browsed the gallery. Not surprisingly, they left with a framed print of one of Tara's stunning works.

"*Now* can we go?" he implored, as soon as the customers had left.

"Yes, yes," she said and ran to the door quickly flipping the driftwood sign from 'open' to 'closed.'

She picked up her keys and whistled for the dog.

"Do I need to bring anything else?"

"Nope. C'mon!"

Sam hurried her out of the shop before she could change her mind, Delilah barking and keeping up with them. She obviously thought some sort of game was in the offing. Tara couldn't understand why Sam was in such a hurry, he seemed almost agitated. He took her hand and briskly walked up the hill away from New Grimsby towards Pentle

Bay. Tara allowed herself to be led by him, enjoying the way her hand was completely enveloped in his but she was still puzzled. They were going at quite a pace, she and Delilah were having to trot along to keep up with him and Sam wasn't saying a word, or even looking at her. Instead he was surging his way ahead, as if he was pushing against the very air surrounding them.

In record time they reached the deserted beach. Tara took a moment to enjoy the view of the white sand and aqua water that she loved so much.

"That," said Sam, gesturing across the water. "Is St Martin's."

"Yes, I know that thank you. I do live here," Tara laughed. "What of it?"

"Have you ever been to the hotel there?"

"A while ago, I once went there for a friend's birthday," Tara said, a puzzled look passing across her face.

She had really enjoyed the evening there and had thought what a magical place it was. It would be lovely to return someday.

"Sam, why are you talking in riddles? Why did you go to the hotel on St Martin's?"

"I went to make a booking."

"A booking?" Tara's eyes lit up. "Oh wow are we going there for dinner?"

"Not quite."

Still holding her hand, Sam dropped to one knee.

"Tara Hemsworth for the second time in my life – and believe me, the final time, I have a question to ask you. Will you do me the greatest honour of my life and become my wife?"

Tara's jaw fell open. This couldn't be true, could it? Sam Kerchavel on one knee in the white sand? Sam Kerchavel still wanted to marry her?

"Are you sure?" she asked tentatively. "This isn't just a rebound reaction to what happened with Donna."

Sam leapt to his feet and took her in his arms.

"I will pretend not to have heard that," he said.

"Tara, I have loved you since the first day we met and realise now that that never changed. After you left…" his voice broke with the emotion. "After you left and I thought you were never coming back I sort of shut down inside, does that make any sense?"

Tara nodded, she had done the same herself.

"It was easier to throw myself into my work instead. Fortunately, it is something I am very passionate about, so it wasn't hard to do. I still spent lots of times with friends, tried to be generous with my time and my gifts but I never allowed anyone – other than Mum and Nick - to get too close. It was safer that way."

Sam had never confessed this to himself. Now he felt safe with Tara and was able to admit his innermost feelings.

"I feel ashamed to admit it, but I never loved Donna," he added quietly.

Tara felt a wave of relief flood through her but she realised how painful it was for Sam to say.

She smiled encouragingly.

"When I first met her she seemed nice enough," said Sam.

"I thought that perhaps I could grow to love her over the years, or that we would fall into our roles as contented companions. Irrespective of her betrayal, I now know that was wholly wrong. It would have been a disaster. We weren't compatible and it would never have worked. I was kidding myself."

He stared into Tara's wide brown eyes, brushing a piece of her golden hair away from her face.

"That day when we nearly kissed was agony. It was the moment when you truly re-awakened my feelings. It was a terrible day."

"Well, thank you very much!" Tara said in mock annoyance. "I'm so sorry that falling for me again caused you to have such a bad day."

Sam grinned briefly but a shadow passed across his face as he recalled the memory.

"I knew then that I would always love you but I had made a promise to Donna and thought that she loved me. It would be wrong to kiss you behind her back, I had to do the right thing. I realised I might have to call it off but had given my word that I would marry her. I felt very conflicted."

A frown creased his handsome face but it was quickly gone, to be replaced by a dazzling smile.

"Imagine my relief when I discovered that she was betraying *me* all that time. I know I should have been angry but in fact I was relieved. I was FREE!"

He shouted the word and Tara laughed.

"I was free to come to you and lay myself before you and beg you with all my heart and soul to give me another chance."

"Damn," Tara retorted. "If I'd known you were prepared to go to those lengths, I'd have dragged it out for longer... made it much harder for you."

"I was already in agony," he murmured, lowering his lips to hers and teasing them gently.

"To do that would have been the height of cruelty Miss Hemsworth. Besides, I know you're a soft touch."

"Cheek!" said Tara and she pushed him away from her, before running off across the sands. Delilah followed her, barking.

Sam soon caught up with her and pulled her back into his embrace, laughing.

"Careful, or your dog will think I'm up to no good and we know what can happen then," he said.

"So, given you're such a soft touch, can you please put me out of my agony. Will you marry me, be beside me for the rest of my days?"

"Yes," breathed Tara huskily. "Yes, I will."

She was expecting him to kiss her and closed her eyes expectantly, but instead Sam suddenly punched the air and shouted:

"Yes!!!" at the top of his voice.

Tara burst out laughing.

Sam's euphoria startled some gulls who were lying in the shallow waters nearby and they squawked away noisily.

Sam didn't notice, instead he pulled Tara into his body and kissed her passionately.

Tara lost herself in his kiss and the feeling of his strong arms around her. She drank in the smell of him and delighted in feeling his firm body pressed against hers. She had always called Tresco home but now she realised that being here, in the arms of the man she loved with all her heart was truly where she belonged.

"Sam," she said eventually. Something was niggling her in the headiness of their embrace. An unanswered question.

"Sam," she said more firmly.

"Yes my darling fiancée," he said huskily.

How she loved to be called that again.

"You still haven't told me why you went to St Martin's. What were you doing there?"

He took a step back, still holding both her hands and looked into her face.

"Tara, I nearly lost you for good all those years ago. Now that you've agreed to marry me, my intention is that we do it as soon as possible. So I went over and booked out the whole hotel."

"Oh wow, Sam!" squealed Tara with excitement. "Are we really getting married there?"

"Yes, we are. Last night when I was back in my cabin I looked at all of the top hotels in the world – in London, New York, Paris. And then I realised that the perfect place for you was right here, at home. Was I right?"

"Yes, that's perfect," she breathed. "Although it would still be lovely to visit those other places someday."

"And we will, we will," he said. "But the most important thing is to get married. You can have whoever you want there, have whatever you want – money is no object for you my beautiful bride to be. I, meanwhile, will be arranging for the yacht to be fixed."

"Fixed? Why, what's wrong with her? She seems perfect."

Sam's stunning, large boat sprung into Tara's mind. There certainly didn't appear to be much that needed to be changed.

"She's almost perfect," he said mysteriously. "And she will be once I get the hull painted."

Tara looked at him quizzically and he grinned.

"Have you ever thought what The Aramat stands for?"

Tara shook her head. With everything else going on, the name of Sam's luxury yacht hadn't been top on her list of priorities.

"Work it out backwards," he said. "The Aramat. T...A...M..."

"A...R...A – Tamara!" Tara declared, astonished.

"Your yacht is called The Tamara. It's a wonder Donna allowed that."

"Donna never worked it out," Sam said with a glint in his eye.

"But it's time it was renamed after my gorgeous fiancée and soon to be wife."

Tara squealed with delight and flung her arms around him. He caught hold of her and laughed, spinning her around. Then he pulled her into his arms, stroking her soft golden hair and gazing deeply into the deep brown pools of her eyes.

"But I do have one condition that I want you to agree to."

"Oh really," she teased. "Which is?"

"That we are married as soon as possible," he said seriously. "No delays, no long engagement. I don't care if we have to turn up in board shorts and t-shirts and have pasties for the wedding breakfast. Time is the most important thing. Because believe me Tara Hemsworth when I say, I'm not waiting a moment longer to make you my wife."

And with that he kissed her once again, so powerfully and deeply that for a moment Tara forgot all about the island and the sea, her friends and everything else in her wonderful, fortunate life; apart from this one, wonderful man. Sam Kerchavel; the love of her life.

THE END

If you would like to be the first to hear about future books then sign up to my newsletter

https://www.dovedevereaux.com/contact/

Thank you so much for buying *Island Revelation*, I feel very humble that you picked it. Leaving a review can make a big difference to an author, so if you enjoyed the book and can spare a few minutes, please would you leave a review?
Thank you!

Acknowledgments

Getting a book published is all about team work and I've had a great group of people helping me.

First and foremost, I want to thank *you* for choosing *Island Revelation* and investing some of your valuable time into reading it.

Huge thanks go to Rosemary for her formidable Editing skills and meeting my self-imposed deadlines!

The fabulous cover was designed by the talented Georgina Moore and you can find her at www.ghdesignexeter.co.uk. If you want to see the next gorgeous cover ahead of everyone else, sign up to my newsletter https://www.dovedevereaux.com/contact

Trusted beta readers are like gold dust and I want to express my gratitude to mine: Amanda Bloomer, Emily Chapman, Justin Leigh and Tracey Smith.

This book was set by Polgarus Studio, across the other side of the planet from me in Tasmania and I am very grateful that I could entrust my work to experts who were also keen to help and guide along the way.

Last but not least, this book is dedicated to my lovely family; for their constant encouragement, patience, laughter and love.

You can find out more about the beautiful Isles of Scilly on my website www.dovedevereaux.com

Printed in Great Britain
by Amazon

62141401R00120